MUSICBALL

Dennis A Nehamen

Golden Poppy Publications
Los Angeles, CA

Musicball
by Dennis A Nehamen

Copyright © 2017 Dennis A Nehamen

All Rights Reserved

Published by Golden Poppy Publications™
Los Angeles, CA
www.dennisnehamen.com

ISBN 978-1-945329-10-4

Library of Congress Control Number: 2016906835

Lyrical Passages by Craig M Nehamen

Cover by Cline Cover Design

Nehamen, Dennis A Author
Musicball
Dennis A Nehamen

1. Fiction
2. Fantasy
3. Coming of Age

Printed in the United States of America

First Edition

I want to express special appreciation to my son, Craig. Creating the lyrics used in the soundtrack of Musicball, as well as this novel, was no easy task. The nuggets of rhyme sprinkle the tale with laughter, cheer and dance. I'm blessed to have been able to bring them to life in the context of this piece.

PROLOGUE

It was madness.

Neptune swapped places with Venus in our Solar System and started to smell like rotten eggs.

Uranus held its breath, turning a darker shade of blue praying that the solar musical chairs would end up being a ruse.

Jupiter belched gas as if it had bad indigestion. Mars bragged of waging war on her neighbors, then threw a tantrum before giving birth to a new generation of moons.

Saturn sulked.

The planet Pluto issued a formal protest, alluding to refusing to grant any future rights to Disney for movies.

The sun turned up its thermometer hoping to kill what was perceived as a potential malignant virus.

Mercury went into retrograde and threatened to never resume a forward movement again.

Earth? Well, we were the ones that had sent our space neighborhood into a buzz; word on the street was that we were going to hell, and might take the rest of our planetary brethren with us.

What shook the cosmos to cause opposition bordering on anarchy, to convince our cousins that we were doomed? That question would have to be asked to a five-foot two-inch, twenty year-old lady who happened to be one of my two best friends. She didn't know the difference between a touchdown and a home run. Yet by the time she finished impacting the game she would have single-handedly given Major League Baseball a new point of view.

Nobody could have seen it coming, except perhaps my dad; they were two of a kind.

CHAPTER 1: RICH KID

As my family history was told to me, Arnold Wolf, my dad, made his fortune in cosmetics. It was an easy decision for him to begin a company making products for skin care, bathing, facial makeup, hair cleansing and beautifying, and fragrances. The products cost pennies to manufacture and they sold for a ton per unit. The only big expense was advertising to build brand recognition, and father knew he was a giant when it came to knowing how to get attention.

Growing up, I constantly heard how I was to follow in daddy's footsteps, eventually take over the reigns at Aurora Industries. I recall my dad's six foot-four figure gaining an inch or two when he'd introduce me to one of his associates. His lips would pucker and his eyes glisten as he draped his arm over my shoulder to pull my flimsy frame next to him.

"This is my boy, Ben. Better watch yourself, Harold, he's a chip off the old block."

Early on, I had no clue what he was referring to but I'd stand smiling dumbly in his shadow while whomever he was talking with would comment to me something along the line of, "I can see your old man in you already."

Then as I matured to the ripe age of nine, it became evident that dad believed I was destined to become a big shot no different than "the old man." It was a wonderful fantasy, especially given that I idolized my father. Who wouldn't?

The man could do about anything. Once on a ski trip, I witnessed him dash at full speed through a series of deep moguls, never breaking form. He starred on his college baseball team and was offered a pro contract but turned it down because he felt it was his duty to serve his country, volunteering for the Marine Corps—years later he'd lead his company team to one league championship after another.

He loved kayaking and would take summer trips with some of his buddies to rivers rated fives, the highest level of difficulty. He also had the reputation of being a world-class chess player.

Once I saw him spread his wings and fly, and on another occasions he walked on water. My mom swore the latter two instances came from dreams I'd had but I was equally convinced she was mistaken, and argued the point so convincingly that finally one evening she admitted I might have a point. "Benjamin, your dad is a rare animal but so are you. You're unique in your own way and we love you just the same."

I peed in my bed that night, waking up from the hot liquid coating my thighs. I was about to turn ten. I remember it because the next day was my birthday party, the plan being that my father was taking all the boys in my class and their fathers in a bus to the ball game. He owned the team, so why not?

I bring up this celebration not because this story is about his major league baseball team and how I was drawn into the business, but due to the fact that it was an event that to me demarcated a reality it would take me over a decade to reconcile—I'd never be close to the man my father was; by most accepted standards of masculinity I was a flop, especially with the girls. It wasn't that I didn't like the members of the opposite sex. I dreamed of them day and night—to the point that eventually my enuresis gave way to baths of sticky wet-dream heated fluids.

As I developed into my early teens, I remained a frail, stick-like kid with as much athletic prowess as a mitten, which might account for why my father endearingly used the word in my nickname—*my little mitten*. Worse still, I saw no purpose in going out and having the bigger and stronger boys beat the snot out of me while my father roared encouragement.

By mistake once when I was a young boy playing

soccer, I was standing dreamily while one of the fellows on the opposing team came dribbling furiously in my direction. As he crashed into me, he lost control of the ball. I couldn't breathe for several seconds and was terrified but I heard my father's voice through the madness of the rooting parents' shouts.

"That a boy, son. Hold your ground."

The play continued while I stood in the same spot, curiously staring at the man who had to be loony to believe I would intentionally step in the way of Larry Simms, a kid twice as big around as me and one I was sure needed treatment for rabies. Thankfully, the referee blew the whistle and as I gasped my first volume of oxygen, I shuffled to the sidelines to be congratulated by "coach."

I sucked at sports by age ten, stunk at age eleven and by age twelve retired from an inglorious career as a listless spoke on any team I had been on. In spite of my shortcomings, my dad still professed undying love for me. In doing so he introduced me to the lone flaw I discovered in his makeup, hope. It would take me years to convince him that he wasn't going to mold me into a replica of the great Arnold Wolf, even more years for me to give up trying.

One afternoon he came home early, hearing me picking at my violin strings. I nearly passed out when he grabbed the instrument and played it. Thank God he wasn't orchestral material…I was. When I was with an instrument—and I learned to play several—I experienced the same high I believe the other young boys did when they clobbered one of their opponents on the football field.

The craziest thing was that my father never chastised me for pursuing an interest far afield from where he yearned for me to be. To the contrary, he encouraged my musical devotion, going so far as to support me choosing an academy for art and science rather than a traditional university. Only on occasion, would he unconsciously reveal the secret behind his patronage.

Once I heard him talking to my mother, comfortably forecasting on my future. "He'll get over this infatuation with music. I was no different. When he wakes up, it'll be about making money, you'll see."

Then I recall more than once, him patting me on the shoulder, assuring me that he had my number. "Son, you get this music business out of your system, then I'll teach you what makes the world turn."

Men like Arnold Wolf are accustomed to getting their way though they're not typically famous for patience. I was convinced my father was an exception in that regard due to the fact that I had been permitted to dodge his wishes for my career year after year. In the end, I was to be proven wrong. The man was about to put his foot down, heel-toe, bearing the fullness of his weight to wake me up to The Real World.

CHAPTER 2: MASTERS OF SUPERSTITION

It wasn't my favorite place to spend a sunny afternoon or cool evening but millions of people were willing to pay big for a ticket to take in a ballgame. It's hard to estimate what those same fans might ante up to visit the clubhouse before the team took to the field. Then, to sit in the dugout during a game—any game—would be worth a home mortgage for the most devout followers.

One year when *The Blue Stripes*—the Wolf-owned major league baseball franchise—were in the divisional playoffs, I was on the bench with all the ballplayers. I'd have been bored out of my skull, if I hadn't taken my iPad touch and played Pac-Man through the whole game. Then when it was over and the team was celebrating, I was taken to the clubhouse. Champagne was flowing, the smell of liquor snuffing out the stench of body sweat.

My dad made a rousing speech to get the troops ready for the next level of competition. I thought of contributing with a violin sonata but no doubt would have been tarred and feathered. Instead, I listened in awe, wondering why these people were so delirious.

Then a couple years later, the team had propelled themselves into The World Series. My dad invited me to come to the clubhouse with him before the seventh and final game. I didn't have the heart to refuse him.

It had been two years since I'd visited the park. I had forgotten what it was like watching these warriors prepare for meeting the enemy. As I scanned the locker room, I was awed by the preparations that many of the men engaged in. Some of it was bizarre, by my assessment.

Bip Carter, the star third-baseman, was sporting a long, shaggy beard and his hair hung in filthy clumps below his cap. I noticed the other players keeping a physical distance from the odor of his body. Even when they were communicating with him, they stood as far away as possible. He had vowed to not shower or shave until the post-season play was over.

Reynaldo Reyes played outfield. He was holding a strange looking amulet, kissing it several times before he finally stuffed it in his shirt pocket. Al Warren put his lips on a picture of his wife and their two little children before palming the photo into his back pocket. Aaron Heisler could be seen in the corner of the room praying in front of his locker, the nook home to a picture of Jesus. A few cabinets away, Barry Blaire chanted in front of a picture of his guru. There were so many guys crossing their chests in prayer, one might have thought they were in a church.

Baseball players are known to be the most superstitious of any group of athletes. From my experience with them, I'd have to say there's truth to the proposition. A pebble resting in the wrong place on the infield can make the difference between an easy out and a series winning single. An unexpected wind can push a ball foul that otherwise would have won a game. A slick spot in the outfield grass can cause the fielder to lose a vital step that makes the difference between a game saving catch and a ball finding the gap and producing a run-scoring double.

Is there an answer to combat the unexpected? Ask almost any player and they'll tell you how they attempt to contend with chance, though none I've met have had much success. Still, they're continually giving it their best shot, inventing new ritualistic behaviors every time they perceive an association between a real event and their state of being at the time it occurs.

I recall a player who wouldn't step into the batter's box without first tying his shoe—only the left one—while leaning over without bending at the knees and standing exactly three feet from the plate. Others I remember would bathe the barrel of their bats in olive oil before the game or swing precisely six times before stepping into the batter's box. Some insisted on taking only three warm up grounders before the beginning of an inning. Others wouldn't shave on the day they were scheduled to pitch because they believed it was bad luck. The list of idiotic habits that these guys manufactured, all with the intent to beat their Gods, was endless.

I remember the atmosphere in the locker room that day before the seventh game of The World Series. It was getting close to the time when the players were going out to the field. One of the leaders, Flip Montil, called all the men together.

"The seventh game of the series…I should be scared, but we've done everything we can."

Then he motioned for everyone to gather in a circle.

"Listen up, gentlemen," Flip called to rally the troops. Once he had their attention, he started tossing out words like warm up throws. The bursts of sound took on a rhythm, a lyrical quality that seemed to spontaneously flow from his lips. Then some of the other players joined in with what seemed impromptu performances.

"What's it all about? Waking to blackened skies…lifting weights while the masses rise. Then after we practice, we run dashes to pass the time. Gentlemen, the bottom line is we work 'til hustle tears us, far as our muscles dare us."

"It there's an obstacle that's possible, we've thought it out, right, Flip?" Manny Fresco, a reliever chimed in. "Still, don't fault our superstitions 'cause tough luck could mar this bout."

Bip Carter was itching to add to the excitement. "We've worked the whole year through to triumph, so the city blooms. Our fans are overdue but you tell 'em we can win it too."

Flip had to put in the final words. "Because every player plays for just this very day, and nothin's gettin' stuck in our way...no way!"

By now the assembly of players was shouting enthusiastically, wildly high-fiving anything that moved. A moment later, they stampeded out of the room.

I lingered a while before making my way to the large box overlooking the field where my father watched. It was an over-sized space. He had invited one of our state senators, several associates and friends, and sitting next to the owner was Bob Arlington, a shoe-in for Hall of Fame when he became eligible. He'd been the All-Star shortstop for The Blue Stripes for over a decade before retiring after the last season.

The atmosphere was festive, at least until the seventh inning. Our best pitcher, Toothless Bobby Hastings, was on the mound. He was untouchable for the first six innings but then something happened. Jessie Martinez of the Red Sox smacked a slider down the left field line, fair by close to the exact fifteen-inch width of the base. Our third baseman, Shinji Irabu, was positioned to catch the ball but it caught the inside edge of the canvas and ricocheted beyond his glove and past the infield.

The next batter, Clyde Poole, hit a line drive and Kia Coe, our new Golden Glove shortstop, simply miscalculated the one-hopper. It was only his third fielding error of the year—a near impossible feat—but couldn't have come at a worse time. There were now runners on first and second with no outs. Immediately, the entire infield and the catcher converged on the pitcher's mound for a powwow. Toothless Bobby was seen pounding the ball into his mitt while the other players seemed to be apologizing for putting him in a hole—they were encouraging him to work out of it.

Their thoughtful efforts were to no avail. After the two mishaps occurred, I could have outpitched him, and I can hardly bowl the ball over the plate. Within about eight pitches, the Red Sox had amassed as many runs. Even with a late inning rally, The Blue Stripes came up short.

I snuck out of the box in order to avoid the foul mood that I knew my father was in. He despised losing. The bitterness was worse for him since he had a different outlook on chance than most of his players. In fact, he had no respect for those who excused their shortcomings due to chance, luck or fortune. Superstitions were the pabulum of the weak and inadequate. Yet he lived his whole life surrounded by those who suckled on the teat of fortuity.

The clubhouse was full of a sad collection of just such sorts. I arrived precisely as the players were making their way inside. Kia Coe was the first in. He angrily threw his mitt into the wall of metal lockers. Then he sat on the bench, burying his head between his knees. Toothless Bobby was next in; the remainder of the team followed right behind him. He tossed his arms in the air as a sign of resignation.

"The Friday Hastings Curse. I'm sorry guys…I knew I was doomed before the game even started," Toothless Bobby moaned.

He'd never said a word about it that morning but it was a known fact that from early in his career, he had a problem going to the mound on Fridays. If the pitching rotation called for him on that day of the week, he'd try to beg his way out. He was convinced that the alignment of the planets only during that specific span of time would be upsetting to his spirit, no different than caffeine caused gastric burning for a person with irritable bowel syndrome.

Had this fact been brought to the attention of my father, he would have intentionally pitched him on every Friday until he overcame the moronic belief, or traded him along with his sixty-three million dollar contract for a pitcher with a less restrictive form of magical thought. Why our manager insisted on putting him on the mound was due to the prior two games being long extra-inning affairs—he simply had no other fresh arm to employ.

Boomer, our clean-up hitter, was seen taking off his good luck beaded necklace and irreverently slamming it down to the floor.

"We pounded them at the plate," Boomer muttered.

"Sure, but they were all right at their gloves," Kia retorted.

"And they caught them, didn't they?" Boomer chided, intentionally rubbing it into Kia that it was his error that started the downfall.

Fortunately, there were no reporters permitted into the locker room of the losing team because the front office would have had, in addition to the job of mopping up the embarrassment of a pathetic display by the team, to explain a civil war. Kia had no tolerance for ridicule. As if spring loaded, he jumped up and commenced with a violent two-handed assault on Boomer.

It took several minutes for the teammates to break up the tussle. Kia was still struggling to release himself from the grip that five of the players had on him when he shouted back at Boomer.

"How many errors did I make all year? If you could do anything other than stand at the plate like a blind gorilla we may have staged a serious comeback."

Boomer responded with a disgusted look, ending the encounter by turning away from Kia. It was Arnie

Spann, one of the most respected and levelheaded of the group, who stepped in as peacemaker.

"This one just came at a bad time, Kia. Everything was against us."

"The Friday Hastings Curse," Kia muttered. "That had to be it."

I noticed Flip never moved to intervene in the squabble between Boomer and Kia. He was taking off his jersey and removing the black sun reflection material under his eyes. After Kia spoke, he casually walked over to where most of the team was knotted.

"Look, I'm no happier about this beating than any of you. But we lost. That's about all there is to it. They were better than we were today. It had nothing to do with the alignment of the stars." Flip paused to look at Toothless Bobby, who, by the way, in spite of his healthy contract never purchased the dental care that would have plugged up the gaping hole in his mouth where two teeth had been knocked out by a ball that hit him in the face when he was a kid.

"It didn't matter what day of the week it is." Now he scanned the men slowly as he spoke. "Kiss your bat before you go to the plate, let your beard grow down to your toes, read your Bible before the game—deal with fear however you want, but in the end, it all comes down to the fact that they outplayed us and we were defeated."

Flip's words had a melting effect on the group. The players, heads down, moping, began to slowly spread out through the room. Off to the side of the space, was a man I'd met several times, Reed Thorne. He was the only person present wearing a sport coat, slacks and a tie. What stood out most about him in my eyes was that his face was never seen without a smile, a sly smirk suggesting he knew he was brighter and wiser than anyone else. His apparent complacency might have been annoying had he not tempered his conceit with wit and affability.

"Boys, if I may have a moment," he called out appealingly. "Flip's right, we were outplayed today. But my Lord what good is it going to do to blame each other? Even worse, why be so hard on yourselves. We had a hell of a year."

Why he would take the loss with the high spirit he expressed, I couldn't compute other than to assume that he felt badly for his men. Still, he went way beyond what I might have expected under the circumstances, especially from the General Manager of The Blue Stripes. Rather than even permitting the players to suffer, he wanted them to celebrate. He was not going to settle for a compromise; he continued his speech, unaware that at the moment he was addressing the troops my father had quietly entered the room from a side door. He posted himself silently, watching the spectacle.

"I know disappointment. I've had my share," Thorne continued in a consoling tone. "But I've learned some tricks along the way. There's no time in life for wallowing in pity. Think of the positive side. You're all rolling

21

in money, young and fit…you just need to get out of this ballpark and forget the whole thing for a while. Come back next year, fellows, and we'll try again."

Thorne then began snapping his fingers, creating a pulse that ricocheted like sound waves across the room.

"Hell, you all need to get out of this city." Thorne then paused for a moment while he seemed to be hatching a plan. "You need to go somewhere that will keep you from sulking, remind you just how lucky you really are." Now Thorne halted his pep talk. He seemed to be further contemplating a plan. "Men, I think I know just the place."

He resumed the finger rapping, the amplitude of sound increasing while he was crafting words to keep his peppy talk going. "Every one of you has rides outside that would cost a fortune. And I've seen some of the women who are so sweet you can't even believe you've scored them. Myself, I've got a chaperone and a flashy home to call my own. So if you fellows want to weep away so be it, but life awaits, go cry your way to Vegas."

The foul mood in the room was temporarily no match for Thorne's brand of comic relief. A few of the boys began chuckling, encouraging Reed to continue. "Men, you've got our whole town hovering, loving you every time you're near. What a wonderful feeling. Win or lose, they still show up and cheer. Now you have three months and nothing to do and a bundle to spend men.

Ah, pine if you're so inclined but why when you can take off to the land of sin? Cry your way to Vegas."

Even the most sullen of the players couldn't resist a grin as the GM wrapped up his consolation speech. "I'm coming too. We'll see the dancing clubs and fall in love each night and morning…and if you've got a wife on my life I'll swear to never tell the stories."

After he polished off the last statement, Thorne seemed to be on a high. He turned to the two players standing closest to him.

"How about a taste of the goods? Who's got a deck of cards?"

One of the players yanked one from his locker and tossed the pack to Thorne. He quickly opened it and dealt a hand on the bench in front for all the players.

"Hit or stand?"

Thorne never waited for the player to decide. He pulled out the next card, throwing it down next to the other two.

"Screw it, there's twenty-one!" he proclaimed as if he'd created magic.

Thorne gleefully peered at his captive ensemble of players. But then as he glanced around the room he noticed for the first time my dad positioned in the exact spot where he had entered. As Thorne made eye contact with his boss, my dad moved to center stage where he mimicked his GM. It was eerie. In no uncertain terms, he let Thorne and the rest of the team know he had a different take on the situation. The man was an artist too? I'll name his speech, *Wolf's Reply to Cry Your Way To Vegas*.

"Vegas, it's a nice town. I like it too. And, yes, you men are rich and healthy. Hell, I'm glad to support it. I'm like your bank and with a shake you can take your take. You might say I'm easy." He puffed his chest as if he was about to blow down a brick house. He glanced at Thorne. "Not this time my wealthy shrew; the bank is closed to you because I'll be damned if I get screwed while you destroy my jewels." His eyes glared, a not at all friendly stare I would not have wanted directed at me. "The name is Wolf, not an easy Flow; you got it backward, buck-o."

It was short of a tirade on the part of my dad, but sufficient to leave no doubt for all in attendance that the owner was peeved. He walked out on the stunned group, delivering a scowl to Thorne's still shockingly peaceful demeanor.

CHAPTER 3: ME TOO STUNNED

What does a man do when he has all the money that he can dream of? It depends on the man—or woman.

Some of the fabulously wealthy prefer to adorn their sitting rooms with original oils by famous artists while others like to purchase giant rocks their wives can wear on their fingers to show off to friends. Still others build mansions so large they can conduct on-going affairs at home and never get discovered by their wives.

There are also those who have a fondness for living in privacy, purchasing their own islands upon which they build a palace. Yachts? I'm told that some of the richest people in the world compete with one another to see who can have the largest vessel designed for them. Some of these crafts are so immense that they can only be docked at a naval shipyard.

When the fabulously rich seem to have acquired nearly everything imaginable, they discover new ways to indulge by doubling, tripling or quadrupling their holdings in certain categories. My father told me of a gentleman he knows who when planning a trip to France was shocked to find out that the reason he didn't need to lease a Riviera home was because he already owned one.

Arnold Wolf? He was a different sort of animal. True, he couldn't get enough of things, but mostly they were ones classified as assets. I couldn't have estimated his net worth. I had never balanced my own checkbook or paid attention to a bank statement. I do know that not long before the time this story was unfolding, it had been rumored that Aurora Industries was about to be sold. One of my friends brought the newspaper article to my attention. I winced when I saw the buyout figure of just over three billion.

I later learned that the company was privately held, most of the stock belonging to my father. It was also brought to my attention during family discussions that Aurora was not his only asset. Yet to know him was to be aware that neither luxury, glamour or fame motivated him. In fact, I can think of only one "thing" he valued for his own pleasure and it had nothing to do with impressing the world with his enormous power. I'll address that in a moment.

I did notice growing up that brothers, sisters, aunts and uncles, cousins and close friends lined up like bellmen waiting for tips to collect samplings of my father's fortune. My impression was that he was aware that these "loved ones" took advantage of his generosity, yet he never refused assisting them. On occasion, I overheard him discussing the point with my mother who would confront him with the fact that he was not only being used, but enabling some of the "parasites." He'd agree, but then go on repeating the same acts of charity.

I know for a fact he put two of my cousins through college. Another who lost her father when she was a child, he took under his wing, purchasing a real estate property in her name so that she'd have income for the rest of her life. The man was like most industrialists, a walking contradiction capable of spawning myths of greed as well as goodness. On the former side, make no mistake, he showed no mercy toward another businessperson if they permitted him to slaughter them in a deal.

For Arnold Wolf, life boiled down to a game, and the pure thrill of making something happen was his reason for being. He'd by far prefer to spend an evening talking with friends about how he made a killing by buying a small company and weaving it into the Aurora parent than spend his time fantasizing trips around the world or overlooking architectural plans for a new estate. No, I had witnessed the ecstasy on his face many times from nothing more than having successfully completed a negotiation.

I purposely left off the above list of treats for the

filthy rich, the category of owning sports teams. The NFL, MLB, NHL, NBA and about any other league of professional sports is dominated by businessmen who have a dream of owning a pro franchise. The esteem is immense. However, I'm told that it is not as grand as the predictable, non-stop increase in value that these assets provide. So while most of these power brokers are having a blast flaunting their team like a charm on a bracelet, they're effortlessly realizing huge gains in the value of their property.

Recognition and status was not a motivating factor for Arnold Wolf when he purchased The Blue Stripes. Sure, he had a background in baseball and knew the game intimately. But that alone never would have motivated him to buy a team. It was because when he took under consideration purchasing The Blue Stripes, he had concluded that the organization represented a rare asset in its class that was grossly undervalued.

The team had been failing year after year. The previous owner wasn't in a position to invest in the property in order to allow it's actual worth to be realized. My dad figured that if The Blue Stripes started winning, he'd score huge on a new long-term broadcasting contract and then entice the city to fund a modern stadium that he could use to glean income not only from baseball but other programs as well.

It was one of the few times that his assessment of a business wasn't panning out as expected. The town was a Mecca for college and professional football and basketball, and it also had a reputation for embracing baseball even more wildly. Still, no matter how much money my father threw at the team, and no matter how they performed, the city political elite rebuffed his attempts to package a stadium deal. More insulting was that the media interests offered pitifully low amounts for the rights to broadcast The Blue Stripes games—my dad was losing a bundle. Sure, it was proving to be a valuable tax write-off but that was little compensation for the humiliation he experienced.

One might now better understand why, after watching Thorne dishonorably trivialize the loss, my father reached the point of outrage. In fact, the attitude exhibited by his GM, along with another factor I was not aware of at the time, collectively had brought my father to a decision regarding the future of the team's lead man, even before the locker room debacle. The problem for me, however, was that my father thought he had hit a stroke of genius, that he'd come up with a strategic plan that would in one pop reconcile several issues that were simultaneously gnawing at him...me topping the list.

One would expect when entering the office of a man of my father's stature to discover an area large enough to house a basketball court. They would be disappointed in the case of Arnold Wolf. He worked out of a space not much larger than a child's bedroom. There was none of the lavishness one would bet they'd find either. The walls were the most interesting aspect of his office. They were decorated with innumerable replicas of products his company had produced. A museum would be a good term to describe it. Scattered about were also a few base-ball memorabilia.

It was rare that he'd ask me to visit at his place of business but he had called the day before I met with him, telling me he had a proposition he wanted to go over with me…in person. When I arrived, his secretary told me he was expecting me and to go in. I still stopped to knock before I entered. I heard him call out to me that I was free to come in. He was on the phone and motioned that he'd be off in a minute. I listened in on his conversation.

"I don't need to tell you I've become attached to the players. I care about these men. That said, I realize now that we have big problems. No, Hank, it's not just losing the series a few months ago, it's more than that." He sat silently for a moment while whomever he was talking with shared a thought. "Thorne!? I'll have a story for you tomorrow. I promise, you'll get it first. Look, I have to go. My half-baked muffin is here."

I rarely traveled without my violin. On this occasion, I was holding the case in my right hand. While he was still on the phone I sat down and opened it. I placed the instrument under my chin and took out the bow. It was my way of easing tension.

"Son, we need to talk," the man addressed me.

His tone was grave, causing me to haphazardly pluck a string with one of my fingers.

"Well, I know I keep harping on you about getting some real world experience; yes, even a job."

The latter word commanded a full note, the bow sliding miserably across the strings and producing a dooming sound.

"If you think you can put me off by strumming that instrument…"

My intent had to have been to silence him with musical chatter, for I began fiddling the bow across the strings in an unruly manner. In response, my dad stood up and began motoring around the office. He picked up a baseball he had resting on a shelf and began popping it into his gloveless left hand. Then he repositioned a picture on the wall that wasn't straight.

Next he opened a box he kept on the top of his desk and took out a See's sucker, putting a caramel flavored goodie in his mouth. Finally, he rested his buttock against the edge of the desktop so he could tower over me as I sat. He took the box and stretched it out so I could choose one—I loved chocolate and immediately pealed the wrapping and mimicked him as I placed it in my mouth—at last, a chip off the old block.

"Damn it, Ben, we need to get down to business."

I'm sure it had to be a mixture of insecurity and anxiousness, for I started to grin. Then the next thing I knew I was laughing.

"Dad, you have enough money for the both of us."

"I have plenty. I have more than you and I and the next ten generations of Wolfs can spend. But do you know what I don't have?"

I hadn't a clue where he was going so I hit another note on the violin with my finger and looked up at him blankly.

"I don't have enough to make you appreciate it."

"I don't care—"

"Sure, you say you don't care about wealth but how could you if you've never earned a dime?"

"I think I'll be fine even if, god forbid, I never end up falling head over heels in love with money like you," I lethargically informed him of an indifference toward riches I'd expressed to him innumerable times in the past.

"Son, I refuse to let you go your whole life without knowing what it's like to earn something, to work for something…to succeed!"

"Are you going somewhere with this?" I asked him; the discussion was proceeding in a tone I found unfamiliar though the theme was ancient.

"You're about to be news, my boy," he announced gleefully. "I'm having you take over as General Manager of The Blue Stripes."

This time my violin bow made an indolent descent downward on the strings, gravity producing an unpleasant and sour sound that might have set a record for note length.

"You what?" I asked, as if I had been moonstruck. "What are you talking about? You have Thorne, he's the best."

"Thorne is the best all right; but only for Thorne," my dad caustically denounced the man who had been responsible for bringing the team to The World Series.

"I thought—"

"That's what Thorne does best, get people to think what he wants them to think about him."

"He took your team to within one game of winning a World Series," I pled, more for my case than for Thorne.

"Of course, he did. With a squad whose payroll is double that of any other team. It is a group of stars that cost me their salaries plus what I have to pay the league for exceeding the salary cap. Ben, you know me well enough so you'll believe me when I say I wouldn't utter a word about a man unless I'm sure. Thorne's dishonest… and a crook," my dad proclaimed without withholding his bitterness. "He lies to those players he claims to love. He's lied to me about contracts, endorsements…you name it. I didn't want to do anything until I had a chance to sort all this out."

"I thought you trusted him," I said with bewilderment.

"A *man* never trusts in the way most people conceive the word," he chuckled, emphasizing the word "man" to let me know there was a distinct difference between

33

males in general who don't get the point of what is meant by trust and a rare breed of man, like himself, who understand what foolishness it is to place blind faith in another human.

"But if you never trust—"

"Son, the misunderstanding is in the word *trust* itself. The average person is educated to define it so as to set themselves up for disappointment."

"I really don't understand what you're saying. To me when I say I trust someone, I'm expressing my belief that they wouldn't intentionally act to harm me. Why should I be disappointed unless they betray the trust I gave to them?" I was surprised to find myself engaged in what I perceived as a philosophic discussion with my father.

"You just hit the nail on the head. 'Unless they betray the trust you *gave* them.' It's all about responsibility. When you, as you just stated, give someone trust, you're, in fact, making them accountable for what is yours, whereas in truth the responsibility rests on your shoulders."

"That's a pretty twisted way to look at it, in my opinion."

"Well, let's see if that's the case. I leave my wallet on the table stuffed full of money. I pay no attention every time the housekeeper is in our home. Then one time, I notice that five hundred dollars is missing. Should I blame her for violating the trust I put in her? Sure, she's guilty for having taken the money. But who is responsible for her guilt? It's me. I tested her when I had no right to do so.

"I'm not suggesting that nobody has values and principles precluding them from violating the honor of a relationship. Oh, no, not at all. I'm pointing out that if you leave yourself open by providing another person the opportunity to breach the trust, then you have to rely on what? Come on, son. If you've listened to me over the years you should know the answer."

"Hope?" I answered tentatively.

"Bingo! You're hoping that the other person's conduct will turn out to be faithful to the principles you *hope* they'd adhere to. And yes, you might be fortunate sometimes, even a good percentage of the time. But succeeding in life does not result from laying down bets on a crap table in Vegas; only the house wins in the end. When Joe Average trusts, he or she is placing a wager, conducting their life like a gambler...and they're surely going to get whacked eventually."

He gazed at me, his smooth lips moistened as his tongue slid across them. I could see the gradual expression of humor creeping across his face.

"Never, never, never blame someone else for your carelessness," he lectured. "Appreciate people's talents. Enjoy their good intention to be decent and honorable human beings. But do not ever put them in the unfair and unpleasant position of having to schlep your fantasy of man's benevolence by you trusting them."

"Some people believe that man is by nature good, dad," I reminded him.

"They're correct. Man is good…when he adheres to rules: when he knows that there are laws and consequences for breaking them. On the other hand, when they do wrong, and then we forgive them their wrongdoing, we are really excusing ourselves. That's why man has such a hard time punishing others. He elevates forgiveness as a high ideal because he wishes to hold out for himself the option to act with impunity."

He halted for several seconds before making his final comments on the topic.

"If you steal from me, son, it's on me."

"So you don't trust me?"

"Of course, I do. But I would never disrespect you to the point of leaving you with responsibilities that belong to me…it's my duty to look after my assets, not yours. Can't you see? That way you never have to be tempted to betray me. It's my love for you that dictates what you might call mistrust on my part. I love my fellow man. Its' because of my caring that I'll never impose *blind* trust on him."

"Dad, getting back to Thorne. What did he do?"

"He was the only one in the locker room after The Series that didn't care that we lost, right? You heard it with your own ears and saw it with your own eyes?"

"Yeah, he wanted the guys to move on without a pang of upset," I concurred.

"He was giddy because he made money off of our loss. You see, Ben, he made a deal with one of the top agents in the business. If we lost, the agent was to pay him one and a half million dollars. If we won, the agent was to pay him one and a half million dollars."

"You're confusing me, dad. The agent must be a fool."

"No, he's a crook but not a fool. It was all handled through a contract, one that I approved by the way. Anyway, we needed this particular player to enhance our chance of winning. The arrangement that I understood we made with him, to entice him to come over to The Stripes, was that we said that if we failed to win The World Series he would get a bonus of three million dollars, obviously not for losing but for agreeing to help our team. The promise to him was that we would be able to deliver him a World Series ring. His career was wrapping up and he lamented he'd never even played in a series.

"I had no way of knowing that this player would have agreed to play for The Stripes for half of his prior salary, just for the chance to win the big one. Plus, he knew nothing about the three million dollars. Reed and the agent had agreed that the player would never be informed about it—which is precisely what happened. After that, obviously, the funds would be split between the agent and Thorne."

"Dad, how did you find out?"

"That I can't disclose. But I will tell you that I'm not filing criminal charges."

"Why not? You just said that people have to face punishment for this type of criminal act, right?"

"I did. But I have a different punishment in mind, far more beneficial to me than going through a court of law. I've documented everything. I can't move against Thorne because I signed off on the contract…it's tricky. The agent, however, is in a tenuous position. He has three million dollars that I can prove belongs to one of his clients. He's soon going to find out that Arnold Wolf is not a docile man when he's been swindled."

"What will you do?"

"For one, he's going to be paying me three million dollars. That will be his one and a half million—and then Thorne's take. That will total three million. Then I'm going to hold a hatchet over his head for as long as he lives."

"Blackmail?" I deduced.

"Never. That's illegal. No, I'm going to retire him out of the business, give him choices that will end his career and leave him bankrupt. He'll pay."

"Okay, I understand. But why do I have to pay?" I said in a childlike tone. "I didn't do a thing. Besides, you can fire Thorne and hire somebody else."

"Why should I? I have you."

"Dad, I never cared for sports, you know that. Besides, I'm happy; I'm having fun."

"Fun? Smoking pot, chanting and laying around all hours…it's time that you become a man." Then he eyed me in the oddest manner, like he'd never seen me. "Oh, and you'll probably want a haircut."

"I'm a senior at the National Institute," I proclaimed as if defiantly advocating for what I thought was one of my basic rights. "You're going to pull me out of school… to run a baseball team? I sucked at baseball."

As I was protesting his inane decision, my father took the baseball he was still holding and gunned it across the room, directly at me. Instinctively I reacted, clumsily reaching for the sphere to block it though it still dropped to the ground.

"There. You're already better than you think," he barked at me. "You'll make a famous leader; might even discover you are better cut out for athletics than you gave yourself credit."

"This is not funny," I moaned. Then, like a little boy, I decided to smugly pull out the last card from my deck; the one I knew would trump him. "I'm talking to—"

"Mom? I already had a chat with the lady and she's in delightful agreement with me."

That's when I knew I was in trouble. Sensing defeat, I leaned back in the soft leather chair, contemplating my options. Sadly, it took far less time than I might have wished; what choice did I have? Sure, I could have told the man to shove it and emancipated right on the spot but…I'll shamefully admit I wasn't ready. Still, there had to be something I was missing that might alter his decision or at least ease the misery I anticipated attempting to be a businessman. I decided to let the conversation play out and see if I could find an angle to use to my advantage—*wait and see* proved to be a wise strategy.

"How much would you be paying me?" I posed with nonchalance.

"Thank god!" my dad roared delightedly. "If you didn't ask me that I might wonder if I failed miserably as a parent."

"Well, how much," I pushed, sensing that bargaining enhanced my position for no reason other than my father lived for the joy of the negotiation.

"Here's the story, Ben. Of all the businesses in my inventory, The Blue Stripes are the only loser and—"

"How much is Thorne making?" I thought that might be a clever place to begin the bargaining.

Rather than answering, my father bent over his desk and pressed the button on his intercom, calling his secretary.

"Heather, get Thorne in here will you?" Then he turned to me. "He was getting a smooth four mil…plus a few perks." He stopped to calculate his options. "I'll tell you what, since you admit to knowing nothing I'll give you a hundred grand…and that's generous."

"Generous?" I retorted with a heavy dose of insult.

I had an idea that I thought might sugar coat what I perceived was a dung sandwich being shoved down my throat. "I'll need four hundred and fifty thousand plus an unlimited expense account. And I want one other thing."

"Son, you've no hand for bluffing." He was bursting with laughter by this time, I believe mostly due to appreciating my moxie. I assumed he was aware that he held all the chips but I knew he didn't want to employ his power and risk bruising my pride.

"I want to hire Whitman and Sky as co-general managers. I'll split the salary with them." There was nothing humorous in the situation as I assessed it. Bringing along my two closest friends in the world might at least make it tolerable. "I might be able to coax them into this for a hundred and fifty grand each. As you know, they both live on starvation budgets."

"But what good are they going to be?" my father asked earnestly, unable to ignore his habit of never spending money carelessly.

"What good am I going to be?"

"Okay, it's your call," he consented with a proud smile.

The man had enjoyed a double win. At a later date, he would disclose to me that he wasn't convinced that I would accept taking over the team and concluded he'd bluffed his way to victory. Then, he figured that the difference between Thorne's salary and what he would be paying to the three of us left him ahead millions. He was overjoyed.

As the man was feasting on the fine outcome of his plan, the intercom went off.

"Mr. Thorne's here, sir," Heather informed him.

"Send him in," he instructed her merrily.

Thorne was a tall, thin man who walked with a stride reminding me of an actor walking up the aisle on his way to being presented an Oscar at The Academy Awards. He was the happiest cat I'd ever met, that wily smile wrapping fully across his smug mug an irresistible calling card.

There was only one chair across from the desk, the one I was sitting in. My father had returned to take his seat. He was reclining with a smirk of his own. Seeing me in the chair, Thorne grabbed one from a small table in the corner and began moving it over.

"You won't be here that long, Reed," my dad called out to halt his effort.

"Good. I need to get back to my office as soon as possible. I'm having a heck of a time with Hawk's contract. Collins, his agent, is a SOB if I've ever met one."

"You can't figure out a way to make him happy?" my dad asked, but with derision. "These agents need a little incentive sometimes, Reed. You have to be inventive."

My father smiled oddly at him, the insinuation enough to excite Thorne's imagination that he might have been discovered but not sufficient to satisfy him that his boss was certain of the deception. That was precisely how my father wanted it.

"But you can forget Hawk's contract. I won't sign it anyway."

"But he's the best catcher—"

"Reed, let me get right to it. You're fired. Ben will be taking over your duties."

"Your son?" Reed laughed, certain that my father was enjoying one of his pranks. "Oh, I get it. April Fool's Day in January."

Reed turned to leave, jesting to my father. "I'll get back to you later when I figure out this Hawk business."

"Hold on there, cowboy," he called out to Thorne as if he were John Wayne. "This is no joke. When you get back to your office there'll be a security officer waiting for you. Take your personal possessions with you— you're out of here today."

It was the first time I'd even seen Thorne without the glee in his face. He looked like a woman out in public who just realized that she'd forgotten to put on her makeup. His forehead tightened and the skin under his eyes darkened. The man was fuming.

"Your son will drive the team into the cellar."

"Will he?" my father answered him.

"We made it to the final game of The World Series; what do you expect?"

"You're out." my dad declared convincingly. "And close the door, please."

"Most of the players will follow me," Thorne shot back like an insulted child.

"I hope they do, and take their big salaries with them"

Thorne did close the door; he slammed it. All my father did was wink at me.

"You never told him why you're letting him go," I reminded him.

"Don't ever give a liar or cheat the opportunity to argue their case, their defense will be worse than their deception."

"So, what now? What if the players do follow him?"

"I've already decided that I'm restructuring. I'm making this a low-budget, moneymaking organization. Son, I'm sick of this team sucking on me like a tick. Most people wouldn't believe that an organization as successful as ours, making it all the way to The World Series, could be losing millions a year; sadly it's true."

"But with no money—"

"You'll see how well you can do."

"But you want me to learn how to win, don't you?"

"Ben, what I want is for you to learn to make money. You're going to study accounting, statistics, marketing, budgets—"

"Budgets?"

"Right. You'll find it in the dictionary between Buddhism and buffoon."

"Dad!" I made what I thought to be a last appeal. "I hope you know I'm not going to do this team a whole lot of good. Besides the fact that I know nothing about business, and Whitman and Sky know less than me, my heart won't be in it. I'll never be in love with money like you. It's just not important to me."

Imperiously, he walked over to my side, resting his hand on my shoulder while he looked down on me. He began speaking. I noticed a sentimental tone to his voice, his words gentle.

"Son, I've got a passionate side. I had a dreamer's mind too."

I was the sole person in the audience but it might as well have been a packed house at Staples Center in Los Angeles. He was a crooner, intent on waking an adult spirit that his son had disowned. His words were presented like lyrics to a song I might have entitled, *Love Can't Buy You Luxury*. He was certain it was true; just as he was the reverse that luxury *can* buy you love.

Love? I'll be getting to that since it's a primary theme in this bizarre tale.

"I loved an opera tune beneath an autumn moon when it was opportune. Those lazy days don't cost a dime and I found them quite delightful. Ah son, I done it too. A summer of Sundays in ripped up shoes...I made love in the afternoons and nothing in the world could hurt me." He pulled me close so as to face me as he continued his piece. "But I learned a thing when I got my green; there's no need for a lover's heart, you can buy the feeling. I love life's precious gifts but here's a lesson

45

kid, you can't buy luck without a buck so go get rich or go get…you know. Come on board with your pop son and we'll shop any shop without caution, get served by the cream of the crop with a lady on top that'll tend to you without end."

I think he was surprising himself with the wittiness of his on-the-spot composition. He was laughing so hard he was laboring to put the final touches on his piece.

"Once you earn a buck or two you'll know the joy a buck can bring you. I could sit all day and sing you all the tales I've ever sung but son, there's only one way you can feel my love for money: just drop that face into the workplace and get a taste of payday. Remember," he went on with a more persuasive voice, "I lived that life you dream and strummed tunes of apathy and it was never as sweet as it seemed. But then when I earned a taste for greed, I fell in love with luxury."

I watched as he loped over to one of the walls of his office. He took a picture from its mounting, revealing a safe.

"Now, I'm gonna give you a first-hand look at one of the most beautiful gifts life has to offer."

He spun the dial back and forth before he opened it, pulling out large stacks of bills. He tossed them on the table in front of me. The man bewildered me and I let him know it, setting the violin that I had left resting on my lap under my chin and tinkering by playing notes that if I could have put to words would have said: "Are you goofy?"

Ignoring my ploy, he plowed on. "I believe you kids call it chips and dip." He smiled with a distinct look of reverence. "Look at that! Trust your pop on this one because son..."

I was still sporting a bemused stare from absorbing him vocalizing his credo. To display my indifference to the points he was promoting, I proceeded by playing a cadenza from Tchaikovsky's Violin Concerto in D Major, Op. 35. I assumed he'd recognize the piece and it would at least slow down his thunder—instead, he kept pointing at the piles of cash as if he could use them to purchase the President's Address to Congress. He was putting on quite the show and not about to let me upstage him. He cut me off, ending my instrumental antics.

"This is what makes nations fight, allows men to change the flow of rivers, women to purr, boys to become men, and men to become kings," he sermonized while still aiming his finger at the stacks of green.

"Dad, I get it," I finally conceded with the wish to make a swift exit. "We'll see what happens but don't be too convinced it's going to be the same for me as it was for you."

"You'll see," he replied with a sense of confidence that inspired more defiance than submission on my part. "Now listen. I'm going to help you get off on the right track but you're a smart kid so don't think I'll be babysitting you through this."

"Okay," I commented as I began putting my instrument back in the case.

"Hey, how does it feel?" he queried me jubilantly, patting me on the back like I was already a universe of my own. "You're a baseball exec now."

Most of the male population would have risked imprisonment for the rest of their life for hammering me to death and then dropping me off a cliff for the opportunity to step into the shoes of Benjamin Wolf. All I could think of was that I had made a misstep. I had all the money I wanted without taking on the assignment and I knew deep inside that there was no way my dad would have cut me off if I had absolutely refused.

Yet here I was, committed to running a baseball team. Not only that, I had two partners I would have bet to have an even lower likelihood of success than I.

Arnold Wolf went off to answer his phone and I leaned back in the chair, wondering if my secretary was going to be the first female interested in having sex with me. If not, might I then at least be able to pick her brain about baseball?

CHAPTER 4: BRINGING WHIT AND SKY ON BOARD

In preparation for college, I decided to try my luck. I, therefore, applied to the most prestigious school in the country. It was a small institution but unique in that it merged students with talent in the sciences and arts. I was fortunate to be accepted.

Our orientation week was an intense experience designed to help us get to know the facility, administration and student body. The final phase entailed us being put in groups of three and then taken to the wilderness where we would camp outdoors for two nights with our partners. It was random selection determining which students we were together with for the survivalist finale. I found myself placed with two scientists I'd had nothing to do with during the initial phases of the introduction.

The male was built like a gorilla and I'd soon be

blessed for not only his physique but also his athleticism and shear power. The female was a bubbly, cute girl who I noticed had caught the attention of every guy in the school. Her outward appearance suggested she had to be the cheerleader type but I was about to learn she was anything but that on the inside.

We all had been given a communication device and instructions on the general area where we were to camp. Everything was going splendid. We had cooked a great dinner and spent the night around a campfire telling each other the story of our lives. It was Sky and Whitman that I was sharing the experience with; both were astonished when I revealed to them the wealth from which I came. Still, at the same time, neither seemed impressed. They were more interested in how it influenced my values and beliefs. They wanted to know, in particular, if it was a factor in terms of my drive to achieve, since success in the traditional sense of making a living would never be an issue for me.

Whitman and Sky shared in common that they came from families that had struggled financially. Both of them also expressed that they realized early in their lives that they had an intellectual talent and wanted to maximize their potential through education. They also believed that it was important to balance their lives with other areas of interest. For example, Whitman was a champion wrestler in high school and Sky had studied acting and starred in school productions.

After fixing breakfast, we took off on a hike. We were about a mile from our camp, when we stopped by a lake to admire the scenery. That's when it happened. I had walked into the forest a short distance to relieve myself. I was zipping my pants when I heard a heavy crushing sound behind me, the opposite direction from where I'd left my companions. When I turned around, I was staring at the angry face of a black bear.

His snout had a brownish color but the rest of him was pure black. He had cute little ears sticking straight up but there was nothing else about him that reminded me of the furry, cuddly creatures that had endeared me to the species as a young boy. His eyes glared at me, as his body poised to attack. I had no doubt that he was in a foul mood. I froze in terror.

I never screamed. I had lost any capacity for vocalization. Then, in an instant I heard a voice.

"Hey, Benny, come on. Time to move on, man," Whitman jived at me.

Sky was only a few feet behind Whitman; both of them close enough to where I was standing to see that the beast had sprung forward toward me, initiating the attack. He raced up to me at a surprisingly quick speed and rose up on his hind legs, smacking me with his chest and sending me like a twig to the ground.

As I lay there helplessly awaiting his next charge, Whitman dove into his midsection, knocking the bear backward. While in retreat, the bear swept his right front paw circularly and caught Whitman across the chest, ripping his flesh. Then the bear stood furiously on his hinds again, roaring indignantly. That's when the even more amazing part of the story unfolded because there was no doubt that we were about to be severed into bite sized chunks for this fellow's next meal.

At the commencement of our trip, Sky had selected a piece of wood she found for the prefect walking stick. It was a thick piece of birch that was straight and smooth. She had a small pocketknife and had devoted the previous evening whittling on it, while we had enjoyed melting marshmallows. The bear remained standing like a giant statue on his back legs for several seconds, presumably deliberating which of us he would maul first. Sky took advantage of his pause. Using her stick as a weapon, she jammed mightily into his genitals.

It was a bull's-eye precision strike, so powerful that if such a thing as a bear cry exists, this guy would have won a weeping contest. He was emasculated and likely deprived of his virility for life. I'll never forget the look on all of our faces. It wasn't difficult for me to compute that I mirrored the terror in both Whitman and Sky's eyes.

As the bear remained agonizing at full upright posture, Sky stared back in disbelief. They definitely had a moment of communion. It lasted briefly. The bear fell down on all fours and stumbled off.

It was dead quiet. We had all stopped breathing,

praying that he wasn't readying to make a fatal assault to retaliate against the three of us. It didn't happen. After a minute, we looked at one another, amazed that we were alive and realizing we would forever have an unbreakable bond.

Whitman was lying on his back, his chest lacerated horizontally from side to side and streaming blood. It was ghastly because the tear pulled apart the abdominal muscles so that part of his internal organs was exposed. Due to shock, I hadn't realized it but when the bear had knocked me over he had used his chest and his right claw had impaled my left shoulder area. I was also bleeding like a kitchen faucet.

The little lady took out her phone and placed an emergency call. She was the only one of the three of us that was unscathed. She provided medical care as best she could until help arrived. It was cool out but she took off her coat. Realizing that Whitman was in the worst shape and likely in shock, she wrapped him tightly to keep him warm. Then she ripped off her blouse to wrap my shoulder and at the same time fingered the pressure points to slow the bleeding.

What she did next seemed like a mystery at the time but later we would all understand it. She took out her pocketknife and made a tiny incision on the inside of her right forearm, enough for a small amount of blood to trickle. Then she went over to Whitman and let one drop fall on his arm, in turn taking her finger and dabbing enough of his blood to merge it with hers. By the time she completed her ritual, we all shared each other's blood—we were bound as blood brother (sisters) forever.

I was treated at the clinic and released that day. Whitman, who saved my life, was evacuated to a regional hospital. He underwent six hours of surgery and then required two additional plastic procedures to repair his burly chest and abdomen. The bear was hunted down and required a sex change operation—just kidding.

*****

It was about seven o'clock in the evening of the day that my father assigned me GM duties. I had just arrived at the apartment that I shared with Whitman and Sky. Winter was begging for a break in the unusually warm weather that permitted t-shirts and shorts in late... January?

After the meeting with my father, I handed in the sheet music I had composed for a school musical to one of my professors. Then I stopped at the Dean's office and informed him that I needed to take off a quarter for personal reasons: I assumed that after a few months of destroying his team I would tame the beast of hope in my father that he was going to make an entrepreneur out of me. Then, I'd be back enrolled in classes.

Whitman was sitting at the dining room table when I came in the door. In front of him was his computer.

He flinched slightly as I entered. I had made a quick stop at the market and was carrying a shopping bag in one hand and my violin case in the other. I placed both items on the table at the opposite side from where he was working. Out of the bag I pulled a six-pack of soft drinks. I proceeded to walk with my purchases toward the kitchen. I was taking one of the cans while placing the rest in the refrigerator, when Whitman called out.

"I'll have one of those, senator."

I pulled out an extra, setting it on the table next to him.

Whitman was about five-foot eight and to the extent I remained anemic-looking, he was my perfect opposite. His shoulders were broad and his neck was short and wide, supporting his angelic appearing face. He wore his hair in a crew, an auburn color the girls thought was "pretty." He preferred not shaving yet at the same time abhorred beards, thus he found a solution in keeping his face covered with a nearly undetectable stub of bristly hair.

He had retained one physical defect from our harrowing experience with the bear, though he only revealed it when on occasion he'd come out of the shower without his shirt on—his chest and stomach, even after the multiple reconstructive surgeries, was badly scarred.

"Where's Sky?" I asked casually, flipping my head to remove my long dark brown locks that naturally curled and then dangled in every which direction from obstructing my vision.

"Having sex, man. She's tired of waiting for you," Whitman responded with his normal wry sense of humor.

"Very funny," I responded, trying to sound indifferent. "She's not my type," I added mindlessly.

Whitman slapped a couple times on his keyboard.

"I'm not convinced."

He made one final tap on his computer before looking up at me for the first time.

"Anyway, she just called. Had to have dinner with her mom but she'll be back in ten," he informed me, but without the flippantness.

Whitman was a complex being. In a wrestling match, he doubtlessly brought fury with him but outside of a competition his soul was soft and compassionate. In a single sentence, he could demonstrate sarcasm, sensitivity and comedy. His preference was to broadcast a cold, indifferent and dispassionate persona but that was a mask he wore over a smirk.

I sat down on the sofa and took out my violin. I was fiddling with it, when I heard Whitman talking excitedly.

"Hold on. I think I'm on to something."

Now he stood, his body erect like a statue of a soldier having just completed marine boot camp.

"Everyone thinks hippocampal deterioration causes Alzheimer's!" he shouted while throwing down a stack of papers he was holding. "But what if I proved cerebral connections in the…?"

That was as far as he got.

Whitman was a genius, a young man destined to make his mark in the field of neuro-physics. He loved studying the brain, knew every structure and how each part interacted with the others, what happened if damage occurred for any of them and what the capacity of the other regions would be to compensate if injury took place elsewhere. It was his dream to find ways of repairing damage to the brain from accidents—biological such as strokes or tumors—or from natural occurrences such as impacts from falls or collisions.

The door swung open and I watched as Sky whizzed in. It was her style to never walk. She moved like a fickle breeze, her slight figure swaying from every imaginable angle. Her long light brunette hair breezed in the same free-flowing manner. She displayed unruliness, her body language suggesting a freedom of spirit. However, this trait was contradicted by her militant discipline when it came to executing a task.

She dropped her backpack randomly on the floor and before addressing either of us, she buzzed to the refrigerator.

"Ben, why did you buy regular? You know I'm a diet girl," she chastened me sweetly.

She pranced back into the living area, falling on the sofa with her arms outstretched.

"Don't fret, darling," she smiled at me. "I still love you."

"Don't get his hopes up," Whitman lobbed her way.

With her head leaning back, she snapped the cap off the soda and took a swig.

"Ben's not interested in love," she whimsically commented back to Whitman. Then she questioned indifferently to both of us. "Don't we have something due tomorrow?"

"I think we have something far more important than school projects to discuss…team."

"Team? Look who is becoming an athlete," Whitman chuckled. "Besides, friend, you can afford more important things whereas Sky and I need to get out of here as soon as possible so we can service the loans we're using for our tuition."

It was true that they were deeply in debt. After the bear attack and hearing the full story, my dad had offered to pay the rent for all of us, plus the tuition for Sky and Whitman but they both independently refused. My friends had pride. They both felt that the best part of the game of life was being aware that you had to play and that there was no escape short of making it on your own.

We'd all discussed that point many times and initially they were concerned that fate had placed me in a challenging situation. I had the option to sit on the sidelines and I could still for all purposes of appearance present myself as a grand success. Still, they appreciated that no matter how deep my father's pockets were, becoming acclaimed as an artist was going to be no different for me than what they would have to prove in their respective fields.

"Tuition, loans, expenses; that's what I want to talk to both of you about," I gunned at them excitedly.

Sky's wrist already within inches of mine, made it easy for her to rub the inside of hers to mine.

"We're bound in trauma but you know the rules, we take nothing from daddy."

"I'm not talking about that. But just what if…what if I worked out a way for all of us to buy some Florida sun this spring…stay at the Ritz, dine finely. And so that we don't get bored—"

"The man's an illusionist, Whit," Sky winked. "You know these musician types, always blowing fantasy bubbles and then slipping inside so they can ride the wind and float on clouds."

"At least hear me out, okay?" I protested that Sky was dismissing me as a daydreamer.

They were both glancing at each other, delightfully deferring to my imagination.

"Whit, imagine with a snap, a lab stacked with neuro-hats and chemical vats—all just for you. And Sky, imagine a closet with dresses hand-designed in every color you can find, a nice hairdo and a lot of rare jewels to deck your body divine. There's more for you Whit. Imagine you finally got with a fox, the kind you dream about, gawk over." I nodded my head in an attempt to assure them I was on to something. "Come on, both of you. Imagine a day without the same old plain old. What if there was something to supercharge your feeling of being alive? Join me guys," I entreated my confused friends. "It's the beginning of a brand new life. Clearly I've sparked your appetites and here comes the news..."

Sky and Whitman inspected me as if I were loony.

Sky's face almost always seemed content, her expression speaking to her life philosophy: "Life's a ball. Come on, join me in some fun." I tended more toward glumness, so it intrigued me how she could always be in such a cheery space. At first, I doubted her sincerity but as I came to know her more intimately, I had to admit a sense of jealousy in that it was real. She simply loved being alive and suffered none of the fitfulness that I was prone to.

I also had to confess, but of course only to myself, that her face appealed to me. Her skin appeared as light as air and I adored the dimple on her chin that grew in size when she was particularly pleased. Her hair had to be soft as silk but remarkably I'd never had the opportunity to stroke it as I yearned to do.

As was always the case, she was wearing her sea glass beaded necklace, composed of amber and tan colors. I never saw her leave the apartment without wearing what was likely the only piece of jewelry she owned. As she sat listening to my appeal, she was pulling downward on the strands, a habit I'd noticed when she was bored or in a particularly playful mood—I was hoping for the latter.

"Well, what news could spark such imagination in my dainty pal?" Sky jested as she reached with her hand to hold it to my forehead as if testing that I might have a fever.

In the meantime, Whitman had another idea. As she was addressing me, he ran to his room and sprinted out carrying a white dress shirt. He held it out toward me while gesturing for Sky to join him in his antic.

"Come help, Sky. This time we'll deliver the package fully wrapped to the nut house. They'll know what to do with him."

Sky took her role like the actress she was. Holding one end of the shirt each they began tying it around me like a straightjacket—I let them make light of me and then broke loose.

"This is no joke. I've worked out a deal that will give you money to pay off all your loans...and when you come back to school have enough to pay tuition, expenses...and you'll still have money toward graduate school."

"When we come back?" the twosome answered in unison.

"You both know that my dad owns The Blue Stripes, right?"

"Whit, who are The Blue Stripes?" Sky asked tentatively.

"Genius, they're a baseball team," Whitman informed her.

"And the news is…" I prepped them with a degree of excitement—a gestural drum roll—they were not accustomed to seeing from me.

"Wait a second. Don't tell me. The mystery punk kid I read about who is replacing their GM…it's you? Give me a break. Your dad didn't get ridiculously rich doing foolish things with his money."

"Well, there's a first for everything. And if I may correct you, Monsieur Whitman, there are three punk kids taking over as GM. I said I wouldn't do it without both of you by my side."

"Shut up," Sky giggled.

"Right this way, friends. We're going to run a major league baseball team."

I used my believe-me-this-time, I'm-not-messing-with-you stare and it did get their attention. Sky froze momentarily but then ran up to me and gave me a grossly animated hug.

"Oh my God," she sung out to the heavens above.

Then she began her performance, assuming the role of a hard-ass exec.

"I'll be like, 'Hey you, over there, you've been screwing up buddy and I'm the last person on earth you want to be pissin' off.'" She turned to address me. "Ah, Ben, I like the sound of this; yes I do. I'll get mean and cruel, the witch you wish you never knew. I'll always point my finger rude and shake my head like I own the crew."

"Aha! So I struck a chord, did I not?"

"Ben, this one you don't have on your violin." She took me by the shoulders and forced me to sit on the couch while she continued her performance. "I'll be fancy and haughty, antsy and saucy, lavishly fashioned, real snotty. I'll be topping the globe boys. Come get my evening robe," she motioned to do it, and both Whit and I ran to get her bathrobe. She put it on. "You see, I play the role like a pro...so be gone before you vex me. Benny, you have me moved. It's hard to think it's really true, sounds too good without even a clue, but I need a dream to imbue...I know I won't say no."

Whitman proved to be a bit of a ham as well. "Um, tell me if I do this right Sky." He stiffened his facial muscles. "Excuse me but I noticed a slight drop in your performance Mr. Home Run King. I hate to be the bad guy but..."His voice became explosive. "You're fired." Then he turned to me. "I can't believe it Ben. How the hell did you conceive it Ben, to get us three incompetents to be a ball team's three GM's? Well walk the halls like we own the squad and talk trash like Don Juan suaves. This dream is going through. It's hard to think it's really true but if the women come by slew I know I won't say no."

"It sounds too good to let it go," Sky expressed her agreement to Whit. "Sound way too sweet not to swallow it whole, way too tempting…I'm way too sold so I know I won't say no."

The joyous celebration over, it was Whitman attempting to bring the festivities back to planet earth. As far as he was concerned, it was all a benign skit they enjoyed enacting for no purpose other than…placating me.

"Love the dreams, Benny, but this can't be. Your father…it makes no sense for him. Besides, Sky and I told you we'd never take money—"

"This is not charity. You're not taking a cent from him. The deal is done. It's my salary and I'm splitting it with each of you; plus we get all the expenses we can dream up. Come on. It won't last that long and the pay is guaranteed even if he wises up and fires us." I paused to present to them an imploring look. "You're not going to let me do this alone, are you?"

"Why would your dad want you do to this in the first place?" Whitman wisely persisted.

"Some nonsense about the real world. You know, making me a man."

"Is there something wrong with that?"

At first I surmised she was teasing me but as I glanced at her, I noticed myself squirm, perceiving that I was being subtly admonished, sufficiently to feel shame. I hadn't the nerve to answer her.

"Well, anyway, how can I run a baseball team when I don't even know what a touchdown is?" she laughed, intentionally veering away from the subject of my manhood.

Whitman examined her with amazement, certain that her ignorance of what millions of people might argue is the most popular sport in America was earnest. I had no reaction to her statement. I was still humiliated over the upbraiding I felt had been delivered by her. Then on top of that, I was embarrassed that my knowledge of sports was nearly as deficient as hers.

"Here's the deal," I finally spoke. "We don't have to win; my dad doesn't expect it. He would like us to make money, but as soon as he figures out we can't do that either he'll send us packing."

"What if we do win…and make money as well?" Sky wondered out loud.

"We won't," I assured her.

"Well, if I'm going to do this I'll be giving it a fair chance," Sky pledged.

All those qualified pros that could have run the team for him, and he picks me. Why? I mused, mumbling something to that effect loud enough to be heard.

"Genes," Sky answered.

"Look, my parents—"

"Shut up, Whitman…we're in!"

"You lost your marbles, Sky. We can't just drop out—"

"Shut up! Whitman…live a little dangerous once in a while. It's good for that superior brain power of yours."

Sky then grabbed Whitman by the hand and coaxed

him to dance around the room. Whitman grabbed mine to draw me into the party. Music was playing in the background and while we were stepping to the beat, we were cutting up like the college kids we were…all of us together repeating a chorus in prose that we made up while parading through the apartment.

"I know, I know this would be the life; I know I know it would beat the hype; I know it stirred me inside and so I know this is oh all right."

As the music slowed and then finally stopped, the three of us must have been re-affirming our bond as one. We were all on the same page, looking quizzically at each other. In unison we recited our comedy line as if we were on a stage of the absurd: "But we don't know a thing about baseball!"

Then for good measure, we did the chorus one more time, laughing ourselves silly. "I know, I know this would be the life; I know I know it would beat the hype; I know it stirred me inside and so I know this is oh all right."

It still wasn't an official deal, at least not until we faced one another, and raised our arms so that the inside of our wrists touched, reminding each of us that we were as one, devoted and eternally united, now dedicated together to our project.

Sky than went over to where my violin was sitting. She put it in the case and handed it to me.

"You won't need this for a while, Benjamin."

She rarely used my full name. When she did, however,

I'd confess to a slight quiver running down my spine. I would have had to admit total ignorance why except that the sensation always terminated near my groin.

"Sky, in all seriousness, my parents—"Whit knew he was defeated long before but had to make one last appeal to reason.

"Whitman, shut up!"

What motivated Sky in the first place, I couldn't understand. Even when I queried her on the point, she had no explanation other than saying that she'd already completed over three years of college and believed a real world break for a few months might be the best thing for her before completing her bachelor's degree and then moving ahead for her higher education. Plus she surmised that she loved the idea of doing something she knew absolutely nothing about; even saying that she thought it would be a remarkable challenge to actually succeed at something when the odds of failure were overwhelming.

"But this is baseball, Sky. You've never had the slightest interest in any sport your whole life," I pestered her that evening. "Now you're serious about succeeding?"

"I don't care if it's a sport or making electric cars. It is business and I've never had the opportunity to try my hand. Maybe, I'll be great at it, Ben. Isn't it possible too that you'll turn out to be the best GM the game has ever known?"

"I'd bet on you before myself. Even so, you'll see we're

going to lose most of the top players and then have limited budget to get others…we can't succeed."

"You said it. A little glamour, a few trips in luxury. Hell, lets live a little, my darling." Sky used her eyes to measure me. "If that's what it takes to light your fire, then I say we do it."

It was the first time she'd ever said anything directly endearing to me—or was she again chastening me for my lack of adventurism?

CHAPTER 5: TRANSFORMATIONS

My father loved a good movie but avoided crowds. His solution was a home theatre—that was his pride and joy, the only material thing that thrilled him. Growing up we had a room devoted solely to visual and audio entertainment. It was a huge space with the walls covered floor to ceiling with vinyl record albums, DVD's, CD's and Blu-ray discs. The front of the room housed a ten by eighteen foot viewing screen, a VHS video recorder, a Laserdisc, gaming console and Blu-ray player.

There was a professional video projector at the rear of the room and interspersed on all the walls were in-numerable speakers of varying sizes, some reaching the ceiling. Directly in front of the screen but back perhaps fifteen feet was a long leather half-moon shaped sofa and scattered throughout the room another ten plush chairs.

On occasion, I'd witness my father displaying the system to a friend or a reporter from a magazine or television show. It was the cat's meow and cost my father millions to build. I'd estimate that viewing a movie at my home might have cost thousands of dollars per ticket, a huge premium over the price of a public theater.

It didn't matter to my father. This way he was able to watch any movie he cared to at any time and without having to be disturbed by the whisperers, popcorn crunchers and nose blowers. And he was permitted to roar with laughter without annoying other customers. He was a very proper man who had immutable rules when it came to social conduct and etiquette.

He loved comedy, especially movies by Woody Allen and Steve Martin. He was also a fan of The Big Lebowski. Over and over, he'd watch the same films and his delight appeared to increase with each viewing. It was not only over a flick that he'd bust a gut. He was known to orchestrate pranks and he'd rejoice watching his fine works of humor unfold.

This jokester characteristic was evident on the first day of service for Sky, Whitman and myself. He sent us on a wild journey, his version of a comical play. However, the man was complex and I knew from experience that every decision he made was over-determined, meaning there were at least duel motives and objectives for what he was doing. In this case, indeed, he planned the unexpected events for our entertainment but at the same time to let the experience serve as a first indoctrination into our new roles.

The morning after I'd brought Sky and Whitman on board my father called.

"Ready to get to work, Mr. Wolf?"

"Dad, I'm not out of bed yet."

"It's eight in the morning young man. No more late night binges and bangs. Tell the ladies you have an office to get to in the morning…they'll love you more heartily knowing that the day after you sweet-talk them you turn into a bone crusher," he chuckled.

"What time do I have to be in?"

"I've never set an alarm clock for an employee. You'll find out that the affairs of commerce have a rhythm of their own and all you have to do is ride the currents. You'll see," he affirmed, rejoicing a second time.

"I can't wait."

"Good. Now, I presume your two buddies Whitman and Sky wisely declined your offer and decided to graduate on schedule."

"Actually they're both coming along. I wouldn't want to fail you alone."

"You've never failed me, Ben. You're just a little slow waking up. Rise and shine," he chirped. Then the line went silent. I was rubbing my droopy eyes when he commenced again. "Tell you what. Since I dropped this on you rather suddenly, I'll give you one day to get yourself prepared for your new role. How's that for a generous offer? And you can give your partners the day off too."

"That's kind of you. So you're serious; I mean you really want me…us…to be there tomorrow?"

"No. I'm going to pick you up, all three of you. Be ready at eight…that's eight like in A.M. You may not have seen it on the clock before but I promise it's there. See you tomorrow."

When he hung up, I drifted back to sleep. It was close to ten thirty when I woke up. I took a shower and dressed. When I went into our living room, there was Whitman and Sky, waiting for me.

"What do we do?" Whitman asked.

I stared blankly at him. "We don't start until tomorrow."

"Damn, I wanted to meet my secretary," Sky retorted in earnest. "Then what are we going to do today? And when do we sign the contract?"

"Well do it all tomorrow. We're being picked up at eight…that's in the morning eight," I sighed.

"Ben, it's going to be a blast," she rejoiced. "I read the sport page this morning and I've been on the internet as well, learning everything I can about the game of baseball, and The Blue Stripes. The team is a mess from what I understand. This Thorne was considered the top GM in the game. The response from the fans—what's left of them—is near hostile toward your father for firing him."

"They'll get over it. They're so delirious about baseball they'd root for The Blue Stripes if they fielded a team of child molesters."

"Well, if this was cricket we'd have a sticky wicket on our hands. As it is, this team is in disarray."

"Sky, cricket? Now you're an expert on all games," Whitman laughed.

"Told you I've been doing some research. We'll figure out what to do to get this team to win."

"Since we have no school today what do you say we all take in a flick?" I suggested.

We spent the remainder of the day in a movie theater, later going out for dinner and preparing for the upcoming early pick-up scheduled for the next day.

Minutes before eight the following morning my phone rang. It was no surprise that it was my father; none of my friends would have thought to call before ten. He eagerly announced that he'd be at our place in ten minutes, instructing me that we should meet him downstairs in front of the building.

We went down the elevator together. My eyes were barely able to see but I did notice that nobody would have believed us to be a team of executives being brought in to run a pro baseball team. Whitman was wearing a body-fit faded limey green t-shirt with, "FUCK HATE WAR LOVE AND POVERTY" across the chest, and a pair of jeans.

Sky had gone shopping and found an old baseball

uniform. The jersey was white and had giant blue letters spelling STRIPES across the chest—the first four letters formed half of a semi-circle on the right side with the last three on the left, the distance between the "I" and "P" lengthened due to her wearing it unbuttoned down to the navel level. Underneath, she had on a low cut maroon top. The jersey was worn out but did not conceal that she had on a pair of baseball pants with the cuffs tucked into socks that rose to near the knees—she might have been a ball girl in the 1930's.

She had on her beaded necklace and had upped her signature smile to a full beam that woke me to my senses—she was incredibly alluring: looking at her scared the crap out of me though I was confused why I couldn't accept that a woman's figure might reduce a male to jelly.

We walked out to the street and there it was, a stretch limousine. The driver jumped out when he saw us, quickly opening the rear passenger door. My father stepped out; he was dressed like a prince but oddly paid little attention to either Whitman or me. Sky, on the other hand, earned a wide grin.

"You three are going to knock 'em dead." He addressed the driver next. "Hall, they're all yours."

I hadn't noticed behind the limo my father exited that there was a second similar vehicle. My father walked toward it and as we were being escorted into our chauffeur-driven luxury car, he entered his.

We had no idea what was in store for us. Again, I

knew my dad was not beyond a caper and I wondered if by the end of the day the three of us might be told that it was all a big joke, informing us that we could go back to school. Then as I contemplated that possibility, I concluded that the idea was at best wishful thinking; never was he cruel or irresponsible with humor and he certainly wouldn't have permitted my friends to withdraw from school and be left a semester behind.

Hall drove several miles, weaving in and out of streets before finally stopping in front of a small red brick building. On a gold plaque near the front wood doors was the name, *Ruby's Spa,* the gold lettering glittering from the rays of the morning sun. The driver hopped out and opened the door for us.

"Go right in. They're waiting for you."

No wonder my father hadn't lingered on our appearance. None of us had a clue how to dress to look like legitimate business people. He had in mind to educate us. During the following two hours, the first phase of our transformation took place.

Sky later shared her experience. She was ushered into a salon area. First, she was seated in a comfortable reclining chair, her hands and feet massaged with warm cloths and then manicured with the color of her choice, a light pink shade.

"Guys, it was amazing," she cheered later in the limo. "I'm leaning back in a chair that's vibrating as happy as a purring cat. I'm sipping this sweet drink that I have no idea what it is and all the while there's two ladies working on me, my hands and feet at the same time—I thought I was going to have an orgasm," she exulted. Surprisingly, I'd never heard her speak directly about her personal sexuality. Listening to her, I experienced an untamable sense of ownership over that portion of her life. I had no right even imagining that I did.

"Then they took me to another room…it was awesome. I never knew hair parlors like this one existed. They washed my hair for at least fifteen minutes, the lady fingering my scalp until I nearly drifted off to sleep. Then they styled me up." She turned to let us examine her. "Well, what do you think?"

The beautician had straightened her hair and then blown it out so immaculately that the smooth fall from the head to where it rested on her shoulders seemed to me an eternity of space within which I could dive and forever rest peacefully. They had also applied makeup that accentuated her finest features, her eyebrows and lips; the color of the latter matched her nails and toes.

My god, by now it should be obvious that I had been trying to repress an untamable lust for her for months. To me, she was a knockout. But the way that she looked that day in the limo, will live on forever in my heart. Still, as much as I knew I wanted her, I was certain she was equally disinterested in me—and it was only going to get worse.

Did she even notice what had happened to Whitman

and myself? We were groomed like dignitaries, sipping fresh fruit drinks through straws while our hair was snipped and our fingernails finished with a clear polish. We had to look like studs, and we were just getting started.

Hall loaded us back into the vehicle and again took off, finally arriving at a shop named *Venito's Fine Clothier*. He let us off with the same instruction, that they were awaiting our arrival. Indeed they were. I had never gone clothes shopping with my father. My wardrobe hadn't ever required even a trip to the mall. My mom knew my size and when I needed pants or shirts I'd tell her...presto there they were.

Of course, I did on occasion have to dress for an affair, like when my aunt married or a relative died. But the tailor came to the house and measured me; magically the items I needed were in my room when it was time to dress.

Now I was standing next to Whitman, both of us wondering what was coming next. Sky had already been escorted to another room. The one we were in was huge but displayed not one article of clothing. Within seconds, the crew of salesmen came over to us and began measuring shoulders, neck, waist and groin to ground.

Then after conferring with one another like huddled football players, the foursome solved the mystery of where the articles of clothing were kept. The space was composed of polished pecan-colored wood furniture and walls. You couldn't discern it because there were no handles or grips to pull out drawers or open cabinet doors. They all operated by touch.

Tapping their fingers as gently as concert pianists, the men opened and closed doors with symphonic precision. Striped and plain suits, belts, dress shirts, sweaters, ties and shoes were slipped on, pulled off and measured by our attendants.

Sky was getting similar treatment. She walked out wearing a black pinstripe suit. The jacket was worn over a tan-colored blouse and the shoes were high heels that matched the color of the blouse. They were made of suede. She was only one step away from achieving staggering elegance.

Hall packed the parcels we were carrying into the car. We followed for the next phase of the journey. It was the one that I least expected, considering that my father had announced to me his intent to run The Blue Stripes as a discount enterprise. Not more than a few blocks along the same street was *Pepe's Jewelers*. I noticed as we entered that there were no visible prices on any of the items. As I browsed, I saw a necklace made of alternating white and yellow diamonds of a fairly nice size. When I asked the salesman what it sold for, he never flinched as he casually replied that it was one point two.

"One point two carats each diamond, yes, but the price for the whole thing," I questioned.

"One point two million," he proudly informed me.

I laughed. It wasn't that the price shocked me but rather than it tweaked my recall of one of the rare quarrels I witnessed between my parents. They were having a dispute over the purchase of a diamond ring. With all of his billions, the man retained a strong sense of value. He had logically proposed to my mother that spending several hundred thousand on a diamond was foolishness, especially for a woman in her situation.

He was advocating for a cubic zirconia, arguing that the man-made diamonds are indistinguishable from their genuine cousins and, therefore, for a few hundred dollars one could have all the joy and esteem that comes with a jewel costing hundreds of times that, and in my mom's case none of her friends would ever dream it to be a fake.

"Dear, the wealthier you are the least likely it is that anyone would question the authenticity of what you wear, and god knows you can afford anything. Let's enjoy it like an inside joke. You can show off your fake three, four...make it a ten million dollar ring to all the ladies at whatever affairs we attend, and we can laugh as everyone ooh's and aah's over it."

There was only one person laughing, and that was my dad. My mother had gone from humoring him, to becoming mildly irritated, to being fully peeved as the conversation continued.

"Jesus Christ, Syl, you women *are* a different breed. I'll never understand you," he muttered as he stomped off, sounding surprisingly similar to me when I would get exasperated.

I remember thinking that someday I would understand women and I'd have one up on him in at least that area. What I didn't realize at the time was that I had larger obstacles to face before taking on the challenge of the nature of the female animal. I had to confront my own untamed beast, an enigma I was still far from mastering at that point in the journey.

Whitman and I selected one watch and one ring each. Sky was wearing several rings on the fingers of both hands, a watch on the left wrist and bracelet on the right, and earrings: that was the first time I'd ever seen her without her beaded necklace, substituting a gold chain with a pearl pendant. She was also carrying a fancy handbag instead of the old burlap sack she'd totted on her shoulder as she entered the store—I'm informed that potato sacks don't go well with wool suits.

When we exited the store after the jewelry spree, Hall ran toward us, for the first time seeming to notice us as humans. He glanced admiringly at each of us in succession.

"It's late. How about a nice lunch?" he posed.

"I don't know. We're pretty busy buying out the house," Sky joked. "But we have some hummus and chips back at the apartment if anyone is interested."

"I think I know just the place to satisfy classy customers like the three of you," Hall offered as an alternative.

He took us to a restaurant I'd eaten at several times, *Azure Rose*. Each time I'd been there in the past it was for dinner. The chef was from France and considered one of the top gastronomic masters in America. Generally, if you didn't know somebody connected to him it might take months to get a reservation.

In no time, we were enjoying a feast, the lunch menu hardly different from the dinner. We ordered a bottle of wine to dull the shock of what had happened to us over the course of several hours, spending most of the remainder of the afternoon teasing each other about our new professional images.

When we did finally leave, faithful Hall was waiting for us. He drove us back to our apartment. As we arrived, my father was standing in front of the building, sporting a devilish grin. Hall opened the door for us and subtly lined us up at attention. We were standing one after the other on the sidewalk as Hall inspected us like a drill sergeant about to present his troops to his general. Then he glanced at my dad, who shook his head in disbelief, not in the least hiding his pleasure.

"Very nice…nice indeed," he commended before deliberating the situation. "Now you kids bring me a winner."

"Dad, you said you couldn't expect much from the team with the amount of money you're willing to spend on players."

"Did I say that?" He paused to dismiss any

misunderstanding on my part. "Hell, why not give it a shot anyway?"

Sky, Whitman and I had our own answer, the same one we'd rehearsed humorously before. It was time to deliver a message to my father. We each looked at one another and then at him before waving our arms as an introduction to delivering our single line as one voice.

"But we don't know a thing about baseball!"

CHAPTER 6: LARRY, MAE AND...
CURLY?

Baseball teams operate to turn a profit, not dissimilar from every capital venture. But due to the glitz factor for the owners, the fans—many conceive of the teams as public jewels—the need for cooperation between innumerable wealthy and powerful figures, and the sheer magnitude and complexity of the industry, the sport realized decades ago that in order to protect and grow its franchise, an overarching authority was needed. That assignment has changed over time but today, Major League Baseball delegates those duties to The Commissioner's Office.

Numerous responsibilities were placed under the direction of The Commissioner and his staff, the most critical being to force the owners of each of the subordinate franchises to act in the best interest of the whole, the core theme being to preserve, perpetuate and enjoy their near monopolistic position.

In many respects, the Commissioner's Office would serve as a court of law, the Supreme Court of Baseball. Thus, the reigning Commissioner might inherit the duties of a Justice, ruling on cases and administering punishments. Where there was a body of law or regulations to guide his decisions, the execution of his task was made simpler. Under such conditions, The Commissioner could easily communicate to his constituents. On the other hand, committing unpopular acts in vague or grey areas of functioning on the part of one of the owners might earn a frown or subtle censure from The Office, the other owners, or both, but no definitive penalty could be dispensed.

My father's decision to place his son and two fellow college students—each without any experience or knowledge of the game—in the esteemed and responsible position of General Manager was at the least, frowned upon. In fact, there were many in the industry that went further, expressing infuriation at the perceived reckless, irresponsible and disrespectful behavior of a man they had all considered a worthy partner.

Arnold Wolf had a different perspective. He was breaking no laws. He had lost a large sum of money year over year. The league, from his perspective—though they argued otherwise—had done nothing other than pay lip service to help muscle the city to back his proposed plan for a new stadium, and to insult him worse, they seemed to be interfering with him moving the team where he had offers that would allow him to recoup his losses and begin returning a profit.

That said, it was not revenge that motivated his decision. He truly believed that it was my time to buck up to responsibility, that I was languishing in school and would make better use of my educational opportunity after I'd tasted the demands of the world of commerce—what drove him was his professed fatherly duty to nurture his son to manhood. Alternatively, from my point of view, this experimental venture in management he had concocted was an unneeded intrusion into my life; a passing fancy I hoped would blow over in no time.

Our first official act was to attend the annual meeting of the general managers. I might add that this assembly of the leaders of each of the teams took place not long after the three of us began our job as GMs. Unfortunately, the shortage of time between the two events precluded us from properly preparing for our roles; except that Sky, unbeknownst to us, had begun to educate herself on the assignment by devoting every second she could to study the history of the sport.

As we sat in the precise place reserved for The Blue Stripes, we noticed behind the podium in the large conference room that there was a long banner reading, ANNUAL BASEBALL GENERAL MANAGER'S MEETING. Standing near the microphone was a portly man in his fifties, Ted Simon. The three of us were sitting alone at our assigned table.

"Change, change and more change, partners. Summarizing, I think we're looking down the barrel of the most challenging year we've ever had. This doping business is epidemic. We get one substance under control and in no time another undetectable enhancer is identified. The public is not only outraged but they're confused—the only saving grace on that one is that it's no different for our competitors in football, basketball, hockey, soccer… hell, you name it, even tennis. Still, we're taking most of the heat; everyone looks to us to lead the way.

"We have massive issues pertaining to long-term television and cable contracts, not to mention we're now facing complex issues regarding the internet and mobile apps. Don't forget revenue sharing, expansion internationally, plus we have to contend with live play challenges. We'll all be busy."

A hand went up from a man just to our right.

"What you got, Gibbie?"

"Any status on the changes for trade deadlines?" the man asked.

"Done deal. It'll be announced any day. If a team is within five days of wildcard contention as of August first, they're locked out of *any* trades after the fifteenth."

Simon had been speaking for over an hour. He noticed lots of whispering and shuffling around the room.

"What do you say we finish the rest of this up later,

fellows," he suggested. But before surrendering the rostrum he glanced in our direction. "No offense to the lady."

Never had a female held a position in Major League Baseball even close to the General Manager title. These men were the brains of their teams, trained professionals typically with elite educational backgrounds from Ivy League colleges. One might have expected them to lean toward the liberal end of the political scale but they operated in a male-dominated world. At best they tolerated the female influence insisted upon by the media, whereby women commentators and reporters were employed. There were rare conditions when a female had been given a franchise due to the death of her spouse. These situations they endured but detested.

Nothing could have been more ingenuous than Simon's statement. There was offense, not to Sky but about her. I noticed when he made the comment that Sky seemed undaunted. I wondered if she had even understood the antipathy in the room toward her being present. When I asked her later, I was shocked by her response.

"They'll get used to me. I'll teach them how."

I looked at Whitman and he glanced back at me, knowing that both of us were thinking with the same mind.

"Sky, this is old established stuff. I don't want you to get hurt," I cautioned.

"Not to worry, my love. You know there's only one person who can hurt me." Her eyes were intense as she stared at me, yet when she made the next statement it was flippant, spoken with the sort of airiness leaving me no right to conclude other than she was again teasing me. "In case you're wondering, it's you, Mr. Wolf."

I didn't know what to say. Even if I had an urge to respond, I would have been too cowardly to do it. Fortunately, a gentleman seated directly in front of us interrupted our exchange.

"I'm Gibson," he addressed to me. "You're Wolf's kid, right?"

I nodded to confirm that he was correct.

"I used to work for your pop; it was before you were even born." He stopped to dissolve the fact that two decades had passed as immaterially as a billboard changes their advertisement. "Look, don't let these guys scalp you; they're ruthless. To them nothing…and don't forget what I'm saying…nothing matters but winning. They don't win and they're out looking for a job. There's little career security in what we do and by the time you get to my stage of the game, you stop caring about it."

"Thanks for the advice," I responded, as Gibson walked away.

Sky's mind was working over some questions she had to answer from Simon's speech.

"Do either of you know what revenue sharing is?"

"Something to do with money," Whitman postulated.

"Do we really care?" I added.

"Ben! Your dad wants us to bring him a winner."

"I told you, to my dad winning is making money. It is the same thing. We can do that effortlessly, I believe."

"You're saying that all we need to do is keep the payroll ridiculously low, and then we just cruise, living the high life for the next year, maybe two. Then we go back to school for our degrees without scrounging like peasants."

"You got it, Einstein," I answered Whit. "That's exactly my plan but I'd be thinking months, not years. My father has his heart in the right place but he's not computing the real me. Friends, for me it's about music; that's where I'll make my mark."

"Why can't you do it right here, in baseball?" Sky proposed.

"Music? Baseball? What's music to the game other than a better workout, a way to motivate the animal spirit? I want to entertain people, make their soul's soar with the gods. You know that. Sky, that's my dream."

She didn't say anything for some time. Instead she kept cocking her head, waving her more-splendid-even-then silky hair like a flag, as if she was trying to send me a message she didn't have words to convey.

"Sky, believe me, there's nothing here for any of us other than a good time."

"Music? Baseball? Skyler Mills? We'll see. You're probably right but I didn't take off from school to spend my life powdering my face and gorging on gourmet meals."

*****

The other GMs had mostly ignored us but as we were talking I noticed Simon, the speaker, and another man approach.

"Great. Larry, Mae and…Curly Q." It was a snide remark intended to put all of us in our place, especially Sky. "I guess we got ourselves the three baseball stooges," he announced boisterously to his comrade.

"Ted! Cut it out," the other man admonished as he put out his hand to shake first with me. "He's just giving you kids a hard time. Name is Blalock, Art Blalock. I run The Cardinals. This clown," referring to Simon, "is Ted Simon, GM of The White Sox."

"Word on the street is you're going to have some prime beef on the table," Simon commented, his contempt now masquerading as sarcasm.

"What are you talking about?" Sky queried in an intentional obsequious style.

"You got an All-Star outfielder, Hill, who swears he'll retire before playing for you kids," Simon gleefully informed us. "Then Wysinsky is opting for free agency."

"Well, Mr. Simon," Sky addressed him, fawning as if she might lick his hands, "I'm just now getting into our contracts so I haven't had time to worry about Hill or Phil or whomever else you've been salivating over."

The theatrics did not go over well with Simon, who recognized, in turn, that he was the one being mocked. He took off, leaving us alone with Art Blalock.

"Your dad did you wrong, Ben. He's doing baseball wrong too," Blalock stated, as if he were making a request rather than passing a judgment.

"I don't know what you're—"

Before I finished my sentence, Blalock motioned for me to stop, sidling up close to me and taking me by the arm to gain his private attention.

"There are times when a man has to stand up for himself," Blalock whispered. "Even with a hard-nosed dad like yours, you have to do it. I'd advise you to tell him to…well, screw himself."

"I don't think so," I whispered back with a giggle. "You don't know my dad."

"I thought I knew the man quite well," Blalock sneered. "But taking kids who don't know squat about the game and handing them a team is downright disrespectful to the rest of us. I never would have imagined it from him, though he's always been an unpredictable man."

"Mr. Blalock, I'm sure you're right about us not knowing a thing and all that but if you give it a little time I'm sure this will all work out differently than you'd expect… and for the better," I assured him: I had no idea how I would have explained it had he asked why I was expressing optimism. "Besides, my friends and I think this is going to be fun."

"This is professional baseball, not a frat party," he spit disgustedly, unable to contain a growing feeling of outrage.

Due to the foolishness of my last remark, he took off. Whitman and Sky were talking to one another. As I glanced over to them, I noticed Thorne approaching from behind where we were standing. He was moving briskly. There was no sign of cordiality on his face. Cockiness was the best way to describe it. He ignored Whitman and Sky, walking directly up to me, the person that the other execs must have prematurely designated the leader of the GM group for The Blue Stripes.

"Can you stick around for a while after this place clears out? I'd like to speak with you for a few minutes," Thorne posed to me.

"Okay," I responded.

He left as swiftly as he had arrived. Whitman and Sky came over to me.

"What did those people want?" Whitman inquired. "You gotta keep your mates apprised of everything."

"Oh, I will. If you really care to know they thought they should inform us that we're losers. I couldn't argue with them," I replied in a playful tone.

"Did you make dinner reservations at that cool place we had lunch?" Whitman asked heedlessly, yawning to convey his disinterest in our assignment.

"Not before seven, partners," Sky interjected, feigning indignation for Whitman not consulting with her first. "I'm having my hair tinted and re-blown."

It was hilarious. Here we are, Larry, Mae and Curly, laughing off a group of tight-ass executives, forbidding them from crashing our pre-season party—except Sky was the one humoring Whitman and me.

As I rehash the whole story, I realize that it sounds more like a Kafkaesque phantasm, a product of the imagination of three college kids sitting around smoking reefers, rather than anything that might in reality occur. Had one of my friends presented the theme to me as a prospective screenplay, I'd have congratulated them on their fantasy and encouraged them to write it. It's the kind of thing that never happens…but it did. The missing ingredient to accepting this bizarre circumstance as believable is that my father had all the money in the world and if for no other reason than to entertain himself watching how the three of us stumbled through the situation, he could afford it.

After the meeting, Thorne, who had already secured a new position as GM for The Rivals, in his typical hurried fashion came up to me again.

"Schedule is crammed with meetings, Ben. Hell, I have an idea. Why don't you meet me at Adriano's tonight? I'll treat all of you to dinner. What do you say?"

The three of us were talking together, as he made the request.

"Why not?" I responded, looking to Whitman and Sky for any sign of objection.

"Seven sound good? I'll have a table for us."

I was more curious than anything about Thorne; what could the rascal want? I hadn't shared the story of his betrayal toward my father with either Sky or Whitman and believed at the time that there was no reason to do so. Then, as far as agreeing to meet with him, I assumed that my father would have endorsed the idea. His motive would have been to keep an eye on what he was up to. Further, I considered in agreeing to meet Thorne that since I wasn't sure how Arnold Wolf was going to dispense punishment to his ex-employee, I didn't want to inadvertently risk any of us adversely interfering.

"Who is that creep inviting us for dinner," Sky sneered. "Gives me the shivers."

"He's the ex-GM of The Blue Stripes, the guy my dad sacked," I informed her. "Wow! That was a rare strong negative reaction by you. Why?"

"I don't know but there's something I don't like. Just a feeling that I get sometimes about people."

"Well, he's not our friend for sure, but we might as well go to dinner and see what he wants," I suggested.

"I'll catch up with both of you at the restaurant," Sky informed us. "Things to do."

She disappeared for the afternoon, while Whitman and I had Hall take us in our limo to a local saloon for a couple beers. Sky had gone to the office, determined to learn more about baseball in general and The Blue Stripes in particular.

CHAPTER 7: THORNY DEALS

It was fortuitous that the annual meeting was taking place in our backyard. The logistics were easier for us than the other GM's in that we were able to sleep in our own place. In fact, the restaurant Thorne suggested was only about a mile away, so Whitman and I arranged for Hall to pick up Sky while we walked.

The evening was cold. Late fall was my favorite time of year. The beautiful robes of red, orange and yellow leaves that had announced the commencement of spring had by now stripped the trees naked but left a blanket of decomposing color over the sidewalks and grassy areas, as far as the eye could see. It thrilled me to indolently kick the toes of my shoes on the ground as I walked, making tracks in the decaying material for the wind to dissolve like sand figures at the beach.

When we arrived at the restaurant, Thorne was seated

at a table but Sky hadn't arrived. I understood what my father was pointing out when he mentioned that what Thorne did best was get people to think about him as he wished.

As I mentioned, he was never caught without exhibiting a glint in his eyes. He exuded a sense of peace and contentment. He struck you as the kind of man who if confronted with a setback, he couldn't do anything other than land smoothly on the tips of his toes. His kindness, grace and charm were disarming but…his eyes betrayed him, a born scoundrel and an unconscionable sneak. That had to be what Sky picked up on when she first met him.

"Gentlemen, where is the third member of your party?"

"Catching up on some research," Whitman responded. "She'll be here soon."

"Wonderful. I wouldn't want to do anything to insult her. She's a doll, in case you men didn't notice."

Whitman grimaced the same disgust I experienced, suggesting that Thorne might be in trouble unless he kept his filthy hands off her.

"I think we can do business fellows. And by the way Ben, I'm sorry about the insult that day in your father's office. I just wasn't anticipating the move he was going to make. I understand now; blood is thicker than water. No hard feelings on this end."

I didn't know how to respond, so I didn't.

Sky was rarely late but for some reason on this occasion, she didn't show up on time. In fact, we had already ordered food before she whizzed in; she looked like a classy exec. She was wearing one of the two-piece suits she'd purchased from Venito's. Her rhythmic stride was suggestive of a female director on a set. She spotted us from a distance, nodding militantly to acknowledge that she recognized us.

When she reached the table, Thorne started to lift up from his chair to greet her but she halted him by sticking out her right hand to shake…with the left she ordered him to stay put. Sky always exhibited excellent posture but I noticed on this occasion her body was sternly erect, no doubt due to her wanting to let Thorne know that if anyone were going to be pricked at the table it would be him.

"Sorry I'm late," she announced with a sigh. "So much to do."

As she was about to sit, she inspected both Whitman and myself, squinting disapprobation. I knew it was our dress, both of us leaving home the fancy clothing we'd worn that day in exchange for far more casual garb than she'd have approved for this sort of occasion—it was the last time I showed up at a business meeting looking like a drug addict.

"Well, you called the meeting, Mr. Thorne. What is it?" she addressed him.

"Right. Let's get straight to the point. Most of your

players have left the team or are about to do so. I'm sure you know you'll be playing next season with minor league prospects."

The waitress approached the table to take Sky's order. While she was instructing the woman how she wanted her pasta cooked, Thorne excused himself to go to the men's room. He returned with a prepared sentence slipping from his lips.

"You have one glove I'd love to have in my field—"

"Okay, you want Flip Montil, right?" Sky noted matter-a-fact.

"My compliments," Thorne smirked. "So how do we work out this problem?"

"Well, the three of us have to figure out if *we* have a problem first, don't we?" Sky bantered.

"It's actually your problem, but I can help you with it."

"I'm not sure I understand. He's under contract—"

"Come on. If you read the terms then you should know that he's under your control for another six years. Unless you agree to peddle him, he's stuck," Thorne informed us.

"You want us to trade him to you?" Sky posed.

"And I'll compensate you fairly."

Sky couldn't help laughing; her display of humor due to the fact that she feared ending up embarrassed by her ignorance regarding formulating a trade. She found a clever way out of the trap. She leaned across the table to put her mouth close up to Thorne's ear.

"I'm sure you would, but honestly I don't believe any of us have a clue what *fair* is."

"And why would we trade him to you in the first place? You said yourself we own him for six years," I interjected.

"Let's not screw around here," Thorne said impatiently. "He's a huge expense to you and you've been instructed to unload big dollar deals."

The refresher drinks we had ordered arrived. After lifting his glass as a toast, Thorne went on without pausing to make a speech or tap drinks: the man was in a hurry to dunk our heads in the pail of shit he'd prepared before coming to meet us.

"The money is hardly your biggest problem. Flip won't play for you. Oh, he'll be there in person to collect his salary but he'll never put out for you. In effect, if you don't show mercy you'll be responsible for destroying the career of a young man who under the right circumstances might become a Hall of Famer.

"And if you don't mind my going on, let me add that your team is doomed for the cellar of baseball before the first batter heads to the plate. Do yourselves a favor and take something now because any offers you might get in the future are going to be discounted for the decline in his productivity under your influence."

"Wow!" Sky shot out her objection. "Mr. Thorne—"

"I'd love it if you called me Reed. After all, we're going to be getting to know one another quite well this year."

"Mr. Thorne, it sounds to me like you don't believe The Blue Stripes can be a competitive team," she bristled, intentionally ignoring his invitation for informality.

I couldn't figure out if she was peeved because she resented the smooth talking, know-it-all brazenness of Thorne or she'd already embraced the team like I imagined she would a child, and thus she was going to defend it with her life. Either way, I'd have advised Thorne to stay seated. I saw what happened to that bear. Needless to say, Whitman and I pretty much kept quiet.

"In all honesty, what you're going to be left with, regardless of how you handle Flip Montil, won't qualify as a major league team," Thorne calmly responded.

"We're just getting started, so I wouldn't dismiss us yet," she firmly objected.

Thorne stared at her as if she was delirious. He took a few sips of his drink. He said nothing for a few minutes, seeming to be deep in thought. He was. His devious mind was crafting a plan to destroy Sky in one strike from his magic fire sword.

"You really believe you have a shot. Okay, then I've got a deal for you, kiddo."

"Let's hear it," Sky invited.

I knew Sky was in trouble. She hadn't enough knowledge yet to make a deal regarding any aspect of baseball, and especially not with a shark like Thorne. Her ego was threatened. I'd never witnessed her having a bent toward subordinating reason to affect but I was worried her encounter with Thorne was about to be a first.

"You sure because I don't want to have you come back crying later, accusing me of having taken advantage of you...or have Ben's daddy thinking I've done him in again."

"I can't speak for Mr. Wolf but I promise I don't' cry easily."

"All right then. You keep Flip this season. At the end of the year, unless you have a better winning record than my Rivals, he's mine, without compensation, you retaining the responsibility for his contract until its conclusion." Thorne leaned back with his hands behind his head, beaming. "On the other hand, if you come out better than my club, I'll give you any two of my players you want...totally free and with my team retaining financial obligation for the term of their contract." His smile transformed into an unexpected plea. "Don't do it, kids. Sure, it's a two for one for you, but I'm advising you like a parent to steer clear, and I'm the one who stands to come out the winner on the deal."

"Does sound like a dangerous offer," Sky agreed.

"It's not only dangerous, it's guaranteed to destroy you worse than you already are." Thorne wiped off the perpetual smirk, substituting disgust. "You three young punks don't know a damn thing about this little game.

Take the offer so I can teach you a thing or two," he now taunted.

"I think you three should know a thing or two about ol' Thorne," he chuckled, clearly upping the ante to shame Sky into a fatal error.

"Oh, and what is that?" Sky's abhorrence to Thorne seemed to be sinking her deeper into his trap.

"College kids," he burst out laughing. "Trying to run a baseball team?" He paused before poetically delivering an intentionally insulting speech.

"Let me warn you. Every time I see a sign of weakness I pursue it. The slightest imperfection shows and I'm certain to abuse it. I've got a nose for talent and I hone into the slightest strengths. For months and years, I've learned my craft and you've worked but a day.

"I'll be straight with all of you. It's absurd to me to think of three young chumps atop a baseball team. You've got to see the humor it brings; you're the laughing stock of the year."

"We'll see about that," Sky challenged.

Thorne briskly picked up the pace of his words, silencing her at the same time. "I'll even tell you why you're the fools of the league. Because college kids drink bottles fast and swallow smoke through painted glass. They dance the night 'til the night's gone past but could never run a team. Sure, you geniuses find a way to pass your tests with but a moment's work at best; and I'm sure you fill your time with drunkin' sex…but you could never run a team.

"Now tell me if you know a phrase from a clause, a trade from a draft. Your players will get mad and you'll just collapse. Oh, there's so much to learn, a mountain of knowledge to soak up in turn. So take my advice, sit back and enjoy the ride, drink and spend and enjoy the high but don't try to defeat me."

"We get the point, Thorne." The man was delighting in putting on a show and Whit had seen enough. Thorne, however, was on a roll and silenced my friend by standing up and pointing for him to wait.

"College kids," Thorne mocked. "They drink their booze and toy with toys and muse with music. They party all night 'til the sunlight ruins it. But when it comes to the real world, they're a wreck." He stopped to stare at each of us for a moment, the elevation of his vocal tone intended to deliver the final insult. "Now don't get me wrong. I'm just being honest. You'd have better odds at pretty much any job than you would running a team. I mean, college kids are college kids, a common breed of innocence. You don't possess the knowledge kids, to try and run a team."

Thorne had gone from a seated position to standing, moving about while putting on his performance. After he finished, he made a slight bow to all three of us, complimenting himself on his artistic ability to improvise lyrics on the spot. He then sat down.

His free expression of contempt toward each of us had to reflect his awareness that under no circumstances could we accept the suicidal offer he had proposed. Thorne smiled proudly as he glanced at each of us. I was too amazed by his insolence to reply. Whitman had no comment. Instead, he was content to carve pieces of his filet that he dropped in his mouth like sacred morsels. Sky's eyes widened and her tongue whipped back and forth across her lower lip like a drunken windshield wiper. None of us could have known that while Thorne was jeering us, her brain was calculating the delight she'd experience bringing down this hot shot GM.

"We truly appreciate your confidence," she smiled at Thorne and then me, "so obviously you'll have no problem putting this little wager in writing."

I swallowed air, sucking in enough I thought I might look like a body builder. I had to stop her, but I couldn't speak. When I looked over at Whitman for support, he was chewing a piece of beef, oblivious to the disaster Sky was about to create.

"My lawyer will have the formal offer to your office Monday morning. In the meantime, take this as a good faith contract."

Thorne took a pen and pad from his coat pocket. He jotted down the intended arrangement and signed it, asking Sky, Whitman and myself to do the same. Mindlessly the males of our partnership followed Sky's lead, after which Thorne had the waiter make a copy, handing one back to us.

"There is one other matter...uh...actually there are a couple other players on your roster I'd love to trade for. I have some damn good prospects I'm willing to put on the block," Thorne mentioned, no doubt assuming he might as well make it a clean sweep.

There was no gaminess in Sky, that's what alarmed me. She was dead serious about what she was doing. I had to wonder if she imbibed the whole of baseball history that afternoon...or some sort of illegal substance. She brought any further negotiations to a halt before they got off the ground, and she seemed to have reasoned through why—which of course might account for her assuming lead position for our GM team.

"We haven't decided yet what we're going to do with the rest of our boys that are still under contract." She glared right into Thorne's eyes. "We will be looking forward to those papers on Monday."

Most amazing was that she hadn't had a bite of the dinner she ordered. However, she stood up after her final words, motioning for us to do the same. I knew it was about to be our first disagreement because Whitman had not finished his steak. Still, to avoid a public encounter, he followed Sky's subtle order, as did I, and left Thorne alone at the table.

I knew we were about to be humiliated, that Sky was well intended but had acted rashly. I still believed she didn't know a thing about what she was doing. What did bring lightness to my being was that she had to have raised doubts for Thorne, our walking off leaving him alone suggesting that he might have missed a point and was about to be the brunt of his own joke. Wish. Wish. Wish.

When we reached the street, we saw Hall's limo down the block. We didn't call him. Instead Sky turned the corner and when out of sight of the restaurant, she began to gaily prance along the sidewalk. She looked like an elementary school child playing hopscotch on the playground.

"Is it just my opinion or is this guy the biggest dickhead you've ever met?" Sky cackled.

"Great steak, guys," Whitman, responded. "Would have been nice finishing it," he aimed at Sky.

"Will it make you happy, if I get you another one?"

"Now?"

"Come on, Whitman, let's get serious here."

"Okay. Then tell me why we just didn't give him Flip now if he wants him so bad? It would have unloaded a giant salary, we would have received decent compensation in terms of another player, and we'd have had lots of extra money to buy guys to play whatever positions we want."

"Because we need something to stimulate us, a real challenge, Whitman."

"Whatever," he countered matter-a-fact. "I still had fun listening to you play that joker, Sky."

"Sky, what we signed has no legal—"

"It's a deal, Ben. You don't go back on your word."

"Well, we're going to get screwed."

"Are you worried your dad's going to get upset?" Sky responded irritably.

"No. I told you he promised he'd stay out of the affairs of the team unless we asked his advice. Would he have agreed to Thorne's offer? Sky, never. Whit's right. We're going to lose the bet in the end whereas now we can use him as bait to get a slug of other up-and-coming players. Listen to reason. One way or another we need to unload Flip."

"We need a leader on this team, guys. We have to have one player we can use to build a cohesive unit," Sky argued.

"Then we need to find one that is less costly," I countered.

"I feel like you both just want to give up." Sky looked bewildered. Then she scolded us. "You're a pair of sad excuses for men."

"Okay, I'll admit I'm not Atlas but—"

"What a confession," she teased. "Guys, I'm not taking excuses here."

"Reality isn't an excuse, it's a reminder. You're fooling yourself if you think we're going to win. Sky, we're up against pros; that's fact. And if I can remind you, we have no idea what the rules of engagement are."

"I do, Ben," she proclaimed mightily. "I've been learning and I'll learn more. I'd suggest the two of you start doing the same. I, for one, am not going down without a fight—both of you are acting like punks."

"You really want to get into this, don't you," I reflected more than asked.

"Absolutely. It's a once in a lifetime opportunity to do something big. I don't know how but I believe everything I've learned in school is going to be useful."

"Well, I don't see how," I disagreed. "Whitman, what's your take on it?"

"Agreed, Benny. I'm a physicist not a physiotherapist. Sky, I'm bringing nothing to the table here."

"Let's at least look at the big picture first," she pled. "If after a while, we see it's hopeless, then okay I'll agree and you guys can cruise your way through this." Sky smiled devilishly. "Until then, I want to crucify this jerk, Thorne, and both of you should help me. My god, we're smarter than him; we can do it."

She sounded like a coach rallying her players before a football game. She must have hit a nerve in Whitman, a giggly one. He pulled out his reading glasses, a pair with a heavy brown frame not dissimilar to the ones Thorne was wearing. He put on the spectacles and then started to step briskly back and forth on the walkway.

"You kids are going to be taught a lesson," he

mimicked Thorne's voice like an impersonator. "This is not a game for children."

Then Whitman did an admirable acting job, assuming the gestures and facial expressions of the man. He magnanimously invited me to share a couple lines.

"You college kids are little brats. You stay up late and smoke your grass. But watch me. I'm a pro. You see I know a thing or two about a thing or two you nincompoops." Whit stopped to compose his laughter. "Benny...Sky, watch this."

Whit had a skit in mind. "Excuse me, Mr. Thorne," he said in a bold voice. "Yeah, son?" Whit again finely mimicked Thorne's tone. "Mr. Thorne, could you teach me to be like you?" Whit asked obsequiously.

"Well, it's not going to be easy but I'll give it a shot." Playing the role of Thorne, Whit broadened his already wide chest and flattened his face. "You have to speak loud with your head cocked back and look like a cocky maniac; and use words like buddy and sonny and kid-o and hey-o and do what I say-o...I'm such a big bad man. Oh, you college kids just watch your porn but you'll never get the best of Thorne. I'll run you losers up a muck because I'm just that big a schmuck."

Neither of us had ever witnessed the entertainer side of Whitman. We were hysterical, the high spirit reducing Thorne's derision to a joke.

"Let's look at our tools if we want to give this a shot," I consented once we all settled down. "Me, music;

Whitman, neuroscience whiz; and, Sky, math and stat nerd."

"I'll start reading to find out what I can about this baseball business," Whitman volunteered.

"I need to go see a game," Sky laughed. "I've never in my life been to a ball park."

"Just remember, when the player hits the ball out of the stadium, don't yell touchdown," Whitman cautioned her.

"I used to go all the time and sit in my dad's box. All I'd do was watch videos and text friends," I disclosed.

"I played little league until I dropped out…at about nine," Whitman disclosed humorously. Then he pondered for a spell. "Just had a brainstorm. I didn't think of it but I know the perfect person to help us. He's one of my Profs. I can't call myself his friend but we are friendly. Baseball is like oxygen to this guy. Let me call him."

Whitman had his cell out while we were still walking on the street.

"Dr. Karlov, it's Whitman. I hope I'm not disturbing you." Whitman smiled like he'd proved a promise. He whispered to us. "He's watching a baseball game." Then he went back to Karlov. "I hear you listening to a game. Oh, really. You watch the games from the Dominican Republic?" Whitman was cracking up. "Well, sir, baseball is what I'm calling you about. I haven't had the opportunity to discuss it with you yet but I'm dropping out of school for a while. Well, actually I'm taking over as general manager of a major league baseball team."

Whitman's laughter was uncontrollable at this point. He addressed Sky and myself in a soft voice. "He asked me what hospital I'm in." Then he resumed speaking to his teacher. "I'm straight as a neuron jumping a synapse...I mean, could we meet tomorrow evening? I think there may be a role for you." Whitman waited, listening as his professor talked. "I promise, I haven't been committed. I'll call you in the afternoon to set the time and place."

"He's coming?" Sky asked.

"I don't know why I didn't suggest him straight away. I promise, if it has to do with baseball, he'll be there." Whitman yawned. He was a kid who I knew was a pill if he missed his sleep. "I'm taking off—need a solid eight...or I'll stumble at the plate."

"Take the limo," Sky shouted to him. "Ben and I will walk."

We ambled along the street until we came to a bench. I sat down, Sky standing.

"Let me get a look you. Next time I want to see you in those slick cloths you bought...and with that irresistible hairdo."

She pulled me up by the arms, now inspecting me more carefully.

"Well, at least you can pretend. Come on, Ben. Let

me see you parade down the block like a top baseball exec whose dressed to kill.

I accommodated her, noticing I was in a bright mood. I took several quick steps along the street before putting on a short dance routine for her pleasure.

"Definitely gets you on my list," Sky jested.

"List?"

"Yeah, my list."

As we were bantering, our talk naturally evolved into a short skit.

"Well, unfortunately I'm a little too busy to be worrying about lists. Did I tell you I'm running a baseball team?" I asked like a stage actor.

"That so. As a matter-of-fact, so am I."

"I never knew we had so much in common," I remarked.

"Oh, there's a lot about me you don't know," Sky offered mysteriously. "Someday I'll give you a lesson."

"When?"

I noticed that sensation again, a tickling feeling, a single rivulet of sweet electrical impulse commissioned to voyage unconstrained from my head downward to perk up my favorite pleasure organ.

Sky quickly lost interest in the game.

"Overall, Ben, it was a good time today, wasn't it?"

"I think so. I never saw you act the way you did with Thorne. If I said I'm not convinced you messed up with this Flip business, I'd be dishonest. But you know, you took a risk, you did something and that's for sure more than I would have."

Sky was standing and I circled around her a couple times while I made myself appear to be deep in deliberation.

"Sky, let me ask your opinion. What do you suggest for work tomorrow? My grey suit with a red tie or should I try the blue blazer with a..."

I could tell that she loved the show; she was totally engaged in laughter.

Did she love me? If not, would she at least light my pilot so I'd have the courage and confidence to find another love object? Oh, how badly I wanted to grab her and pull her tiny lips to mine, telling her of the passionate love I wanted to make to her—all I did was start strolling down the block with her by my side. It never dawned on me to wonder if she was as frustrated as I.

CHAPTER 8: RIPLEY'S, BELIEVE IT OR NOT

There was a large sign hanging a few feet behind the bar. It illuminated in bright red letters, *Ripley's*. The three of us were working on a beer, Sky shuffling through a stack of papers. Since the manager's meeting, she had been dedicating herself feverishly to prepare for the beginning of spring training; the opening of camp was just around the corner. For the new GMs at Ripley's there was loud music playing, making it necessary to raise our voices. Sky picked up a thick book and held it out for us to see.

"This entire volume, fellows, is about league rules." She opened to a page she'd marked. "This chapter is on salaries. Get this, the league office can in some cases object to a contract negotiation. They also handle arbitrations." She flipped to another page. "This here covers

The Commissioner's Office and the powers and responsibilities of The Commissioner."

"Definitely heavyweight material," I commented as I hoisted a second book she had in front of her.

"More heavy than you'd imagine. The television rights alone are worth billions of dollars. We're dealing with a giant industry here. You're dad's given us a chance to go straight to the big leagues," Sky exulted.

"This is better than sex for you, isn't it, Sky?" Whitman surmised as he witnessed her enthusiasm.

Before answering she glanced in my direction, reigniting that familiar quiver for me.

"I'm not sure yet."

Then Sky did the funniest thing. She turned her head toward Whitman, pointing with her right index finger to her buttocks as she bent over.

"By next year's annual meeting I want those managers standing in line begging to place their sweet lips… right around here." She touched her butt cheek at the same time she puckered her facial lips.

Whitman downed his beer. "We turn this team into a winner and I'll be the first in line," he grinned.

"Whitman, I'll be sure to remember that."

"The way things are going, Whit, I don't believe you have much to worry about," I interjected, but not without immediately knowing I might have done better for myself by shutting up.

"Neither of you virile male geniuses have any ideas

how we're going to make history?" she posed, ignoring my unnecessary negativity.

"I'm working on it," Whitman said dispassionately.

"In case either of you are interested, we…well, I have already made history."

"How is that?" Whitman gratified her by asking.

"I'm the first female GM ever for a major league team."

"Well, if we don't find a miracle solution for bringing this team around, I'm confident you'll also become the shortest tenured GM in baseball history. I'm thinking," Whitman mentioned in the deeply introspective manner I recognized would occur when he was sinking his teeth into a challenging problem. "Baseball is no different than anything else; there is always a way to take it to a new level, something that's never been tried before. Benny, let's find it because if we don't Sky is going to cry. Besides, I like the idea of biting down on her ass."

"I spent some time on the web last night looking into the history of motivational, inspirational and team building approaches that have been used by various teams. There's nothing novel there," I informed my surprised partners.

"Something new. It has to be. We can't think like our competition," Sky mused.

I noticed after we settled at our table that the waitress had aroused Whitman's attention. He couldn't take his eyes off her and when we ordered beers he did the best he could to flirt; his curse was that he was as retarded as I at getting girls. He needed one that would do the heavy lifting for him, one with the visual power to recognize the genius of his mind and excuse the timidity of his heart.

We were sitting with empty glasses when she approached us for the second time. She was an exotic girl—Polynesian no doubt—wearing a skimpy and provocative outfit. When she came to our table she placed her serving tray down and took a step backward, pointing at Whitman. I watched as his eyes widened.

"Every so often we have a waitress choice night, we get to pick a man to dance with." She held out her hand to Whitman. "Come dance with me?"

Whitman's mouth dropped to his toes. I noticed his head bobbing like one of the undamped vibrations he babbled about from time to time when discussing aspects of physics, what he referred to as a type of movement that never loses energy—his chin was oscillating wildly within about a three-degree arc. Finally he lifted his body, as if he were under her command. I'll hand it to him, he went out on the dance floor and with the good fortune of a slow beat he embraced her like a champ.

"I know who you are," the girl named Kona informed him. "I recognized all three of you from that picture in the paper the other day.

"I didn't know we were so famous."

"See that screen there?" Kona asked as she pointed to

a movie-sized television. "When The Blue Stripes play it's on. We're so packed at those times you could pass out cold and never hit the ground."

"You might be the best looking girl I've ever seen," Whitman swooned, indifferent to her baseball message.

"Bring me a winning team…what's your name?"

"Whitman. Once in a while they call me Whit."

"Whit, The Blue Stripes win this year and I swear on the soul of the magical Mauna Kea…"

She then craned her neck so that her lips were close enough to nibble on his ear. She whispered her next statement, one that caused Whitman to go weak at the knees. Later, much later, he'd disclose to me that the message she gave him was to the effect that if The Blue Stripes were winners she was going to screw him silly. At the time she spoke those words, I was observing them on the dance floor and noticed Whitman flush.

"Oh my god," was all he managed to squeak back to her.

"It's up to you, Whit," Kona expressed to assure him she was earnest.

"You really look fine," Whitman panted.

"I'm concerned, Whit. I have to be honest. Word on the street is that you and your buddies don't know a slider from a fastball; you're all ignorant about running The Stripes."

"I'm learning," Whitman answered as if begging.

"I'll give you a lesson, school boy. Our city is

depressed. We've got a city administrator who was just convicted of embezzlement and half of the people have no jobs. Hell, crime is so bad the crooks have to carry pepper spray." Kona was holding him around the waist but leaned back to be sure she was looking directly into his eyes. "Whitman, with that said, during baseball season it's all okay. Then when we're winning...none of the heartache matters."

"The team doesn't pay people's bills," Whitman answered sensibly.

"Pays mine. More customers, more tips. Happy customers when the team is thriving and the tips get even larger. A world championship and I retire."

"Still, if people don't have much money."

Kona, still looking at him, started laughing. "When you're in love, money doesn't matter."

It was definitely a different philosophy than that of Arnold Wolf; he argued that the pocketbook always prevailed and without a buck in hand, love had no more heart than a bill collector—at that moment Whitman didn't give a wit about differing views on love and money.

"I don't think I've ever been in love," he responded as if mesmerized.

"I'm your love machine," Kona chuckled. "Let me show you why that job of *yours* is no joke."

They had been standing, hardly moving. Still, the slow rhythm of the song permitted them to hold one another while talking. But as Kona completed her last sentence a new, more upbeat, faster-paced piece began playing. The crowd had thickened since we had arrived and more of the young customers were feeling their brew.

Kona broke the embrace with Whitman. He watched as she ran over to the bar and then jumped atop, standing in front of the crowd. She motioned to the bartender, who casually handed her a mug of beer. She held it aloft, taking a chug before calling out to the patrons.

"Anyone ready for a baseball season?"

There was loud roaring from the group.

"And we fight for who?" she called out.

"The Blue Stripes," the entire bar responded back to her.

By then four other waitresses, dressed identically to Kona, stood on the bar, two on each side of her.

"I'll drink to that," Kona yelled as she downed another gulp of beer.

Kona assumed the lead in singing a song I presumed was called *Through Thick and Thunder*. I can't recall all of the lyrics but I'll do my best to paraphrase. *You see the city sleeps most of the year; people stay huddled in their homes and the nights are lifeless. The winters freeze us and they often leave us in a saddened solemn mood that draws us home in somber. But when we've lost all passion we still find satisfaction in our silly springtime hope that we may house a champion.*

The chorus was repeated throughout the song and spoke to *crying, vying and cringing for them, fighting for our Stripes through the thick and the thunder.*

Then the stanzas continued:

But remember, it's not always such a glorious summer. The thick gets awful thick. When the team's a wreck headed straight from par to dreck, the winter's woeful tune just gives its way to sunny gloom. And a heavy feel takes hold when the season's sealed. So we make our humble appeal and beg of you to share some zeal. And spark our passion, drive us from inaction, wake our silly springtime hope that we may house a champion.

Kona pointed directly at Whitman when she sang the next stanza.

So bear our weight 'cause that's the job you chose to take. Think of all the times we cheer as inspiration dear... to spark our passion.

Finally, locking in on her visual embrace of Whitman and speaking directly at him, she had to have adlibbed a final line: *Do you want my passion?*

Every person in the bar was singing along. The peppy chorus was repeated innumerable times, Kona using it to bring the crowd to a frenzy—Sky and I were gaping at the pandemonium.

As the music gradually came to an end, the bar filled with background sound. Kona made her way to Whitman.

"Get the point?"

"I should have been a baseball player," Whitman joked.

"You come see me after the season if you put together a winning ticket and you'll know what it's like to be one...I promise."

Kona resumed her duties and Whitman returned to Sky and me.

"These people are crazed about our team," Sky said with amazement.

"Sky, baseball's the most indestructible sport in America. These people are the reason," Whitman explained.

"Good to know our market," Sky calculated. "Now, what did that girl say to you?"

"It was nothing."

"Nothing! That was not nothing," I teased.

"You told me, Ben, that with this new job we'd get women."

"Did I?"

"I love this," Whitman elated.

"I thought we were here to work," Sky reminded us.

"Actually, I was just thinking about something" Whitman mentioned, as my cell went off.

"Hello...Mr. Thorne?" I answered while at the same time motioning for Whitman to wait. "Sure, we'll have it by Wednesday," I responded. "You want to meet then." I voiced his words so that Whitman and Sky could hear. "That'll be fine."

"Something to look forward to," Sky said sarcastically.

"Whitman, you were about to say something."

"Right, Ben...but wait," he responded excitedly as he peered across the room. "Professor Karlov, Professor Karlov," he shouted through the bar.

Karlov responded to his name by ponderously rotating his body several full revolutions. The man's odd movement allowed both Sky and me to recognize him as the object of Whitman's exclamation. He appeared lost, standing in one spot as if spinning in space.

My first impression of the man was unforgettable. He truly seemed as if he hadn't yet awakened, not to the day itself but rather to a greater connectedness to life. His dress and attention to elemental aspects of appearance was deplorable. He was wearing a pair of black and white plaid baggy pants and a yellow short-sleeved shirt. Making his presentation all the more characteristic of a clown were the black suspenders he had the good sense to wear for it was obvious that without them he'd have been raw-assed.

Whitman, brought to hysteria watching his true genius professor unable to break the gyroscopic force holding him in place, finally ran over to him and mercifully led the man to our table. He had to be in his early forties though he looked like a child. His hair was sandy-brown in color and the long curls hung randomly in every which direction, making my similar style locks seem orderly. He giggled far more than I did.

"Professor, these are my best friends…and business associates, Ben and Sky."

Karlov nodded as if trying to calculate how many different hands could be dealt from a single deck of cards. Then he scanned the room until he caught the attention of one of the waitresses, by chance Kona. He motioned for her to come to the table.

"Whatever they're drinking, another round. I'll take a double martini…very dry; cleans the palate before drinking. Back it up with a Jim Beam, neat. I'll mix the coke myself," Karlov instructed.

"Ben here, his last name is…Wolf," Whitman mentioned, moving close to Karlov to be sure the man heard him. When he was convinced Karlov had not, he emphasized the point. "Sir, that's like W O L F." He slowly spelled my last name.

Karlov remained inattentive, instead seeming to be following the waitress as she was entering her order. Then he stood and disappeared, not returning for several minutes.

"What happened to you?" Whitman asked his professor.

"Bathroom," Karlov replied, his parsimony not owing so much to a wish to conserve words as part of a quirky style of expression.

"I was asking you before you left, if W O L F means anything to you?" Whitman slowly repeated the letters.

"FLOW, spelled backwards," Karlov whimsically

replied, reminding me that my father had made the same reverse letter association the day of the World Series.

"It's also, Wolf, like in owner of The Blue Stripes."

Finally Karlov displayed recognition, quickly jerking his head in my direction.

"Ben here is the guy Mr. Wolf turned the team over to. Then Ben asked Sky and I to help him. We're GMs of The Blue Stripes," Whitman heralded.

Karlov bowed his head, closed his eyes, and seemed to be in communion before finally speaking.

"I have degrees from Cal Tech and Harvard. I teach at The National Institute. I've studied baseball, written articles on baseball statistics and..."

Kona was holding a platter filled with drinks and when he saw her he ceased talking. She placed the glasses on the table, the correct ones in front of each of us.

"There. That ought to hold you," Kona smiled.

"If you wouldn't mind...don't rush off too fast now. What do you say...well; cover me with two more Jims. Just want to have them handy," Karlov ordered with businesslike formality.

I noticed that his speech lacked fluidity. More often he'd speak in abbreviated bursts, frequently abruptly cutting off a phrase. Then at other times he'd meander, talking in dull prose.

Kona no doubt recognized she was dealing with a strange bird and took the liberty to wittily tease him.

"That's all?"

"For now, but let me know…uh, yeah, don't go on break without checking with me." As she left the table, Karlov labored to poke his recall. "Where was I? Oh, right. GMs, all of you." His mind was searching for a principle or category to comprehend the strange circumstance and then store the confounding piece of data. "I've contacted every team in the country trying to get a consulting gig. For Christ sakes, I've never even gotten a rotten rejection letter. And this kid gets a team…without doing a thing?"

The thought deserved more than a sip. He took the martini and downed it.

"He's a rich kid and life's not fair," Sky gently imposed on him. "Gotta get over that sort of stuff."

"Girlie, I'll be brutally honest. My career bores me; and I can't for the life of me figure out why I can't get a job in baseball. My romantic life is a disaster. I recently had my fortieth birthday and I couldn't even get a date. I can't get over it," he yelled out to be certain he was heard over the din of the background music.

Making his lamentation all the more believable was his tugging on the short tie he wore around his neck. It was plain white in color but further confirmed his lack of taste in that he'd tied it so that it fell to the level of his lower chest; with his pants pulled up above his navel his presentation unabashedly announced him as a dork.

"We might be able to solve your career problem. We need your help," Sky informed him.

"Help with what?"

In response to his question, we all looked at each other and nodded our heads, a cue prompting us to stand and comically speak as one voice.

"We don't know a thing about baseball."

Karlov shook his head, trying to make sense of what he was hearing. To aid comprehension, he poured coke in the Jim Beam and took it down like a glass filled with medicine.

"You'll fit right in," he flipped at us. "None of the team execs seem to know what they're doing either."

"Well, will you help us?" we asked tentatively.

"You're serious?"

Karlov picked up the glass that had contained the Jim and was about to take it in one large gulp before he realized it was empty. Then he pointed to our glasses.

"Aren't you kids drinking?"

None of us said a word. As absurd as Karlov appeared, if Whitman was endorsing him as a baseball genius we were more interested in landing him to assist us than getting slammed. Kona made a quick stop, depositing the two added drinks Karlov had ordered. As he reached for one of them, by chance his hand knocked over a glass of water.

"Error! Error! Error!" he cried out, gesturing to the fallen glass.

"It's nothing," Sky said reassuringly. "We can wipe it up."

"Errors. Can't afford errors on your team," he educated us, as he took yet another drink while Kona wiped the table dry. "You kids have Paul House playing second base for you. Last year he made thirty-one fielding errors resulting in twenty-two unearned runs for your opponents.

"That's the beginning. Every error he made took an out away from a pitcher, increased the pitch count unnecessarily. Then his bat was flat all year; he drove in a measly forty-one runs. If every one of your players had been as unproductive as House, you would have had a net four-hundred and seventy-three runs less than your competitors over the course of the season, and you would have lost about one hundred and two games. In other words, you'd have been the absolute worst team in baseball."

Karlov had perked up. He was extraordinarily alert whereas moments before one might have thought he was slumberous. Was it the drink or the thrill of discussing baseball? I watched him taking down shots on many occasions after my first introduction to him. It didn't matter how much alcohol he consumed, he retained perfect cognition and his affect was steady with or without drinking. I had to conclude that what aroused this man's soul was purely baseball; he was a freak for the game, precisely as Whitman had promoted him.

After lecturing on the liability of having House play for The Blue Stripes, he whooped loud enough to be heard across the bar, quite an accomplishment given that the employees had to be candidates for hearing aids once their career at the saloon ended.

"How much did House make last year?"

Kona was patrolling in our vicinity. She heard his question and immediately loped over to the table, relieving Whitman and I of being embarrassed that we didn't know.

"Seven and a half mil," she confidently responded.

"You are correct! My next drink is on you," he jested. "It's ridiculous."

"I did notice that House is under contract—"Sky tried to interject.

"Dump him! Find a team without retrograde amnesia, one that can remember what he was like in his prime. There are lots of morons out there who will pay, hoping they can revive his talent." Karlov stopped to shake his head in disbelief of what he knew was a truism. "Unload him and his contract for the next four years on some nostalgic illusionist. That's making a deal," he pronounced sonorously.

"Another problem we have is we don't have much money," Sky confessed.

"No money, no win," he flatly informed her.

"We want to win. We're searching for something

that's never been tried before. There has to be a novel approach to baseball," Sky posited.

"Try counterfeiting," Karlov off-handedly jabbered. "By the way, all this advice doesn't come cheap," he quipped.

"I did notice we have some budget for—"

"Only joking, my lady. Money's not my faith. My religion, baseball." Karlov then proceeded with what might have passed on a Sunday as an evangelical gospel sermon. "I attend The Blue Stripes' games like a true devotee. I study the game's statistics like a believer imbibes the bible. I atone for my team's losses like a sinner goes to a confessional. I pray for the victories of my team like a god-fearing soul prostrate at the Gates of Heaven. All I ask is to be delivered—"

"Professor, professor," Sky interrupted to calm him. "Will a seat in our box help?"

"I'm your servant," Karlov answered obsequiously.

"Professor!" I had yet another item on our laundry list. "What happened was that Thorne wanted Flip Montil but we refused initially giving him up until we had an idea what he was worth. At the same time, given the monetary restraints my father placed on us, we knew we couldn't keep his huge contract."

"Makes sense so far."

"So you see," I went on tentatively, "we ended up making a deal with Thorne. If we don't beat his team's record this season he gets Flip at the end of the year, without any compensation. If we do beat his team then we get any two of his players we choose, free."

"That was bad. He just routed out your rectum with a blow torch."

"Aren't there things—?'

"Look, kids. You all strike me pretty much as nerds. Since I'm definitely one too, I'll speak to you in terms of science. You can't make water without a couple 'H's and an 'O.' Likewise you can't win at baseball without the smarts to select the players that will beat the statistics in ways that produce net runs."

Karlov stood to leave. Astonishingly, he was as sober as a nun.

"I wish you luck but contrary to popular opinion, there's very little of the element of chance in baseball. It's about money and knowing how to spend it wisely. Sure, you can win on a lower budget sometimes but only if you know how to get cheap players capable of scoring and keeping the other teams from bringing in runs. Simple, isn't it?"

"Far from it," Sky mused. "It sounds highly complex but I still say we have to gain our advantage in some unique manner. Now, can we call you again?"

"Sure, call me whatever you want," he laughed. "Call me a truck, call me a bus, call me an airplane, call me a car—make it a Rolls if you do." He took off as deliriously as he'd arrived.

I thought Karlov contradicted himself, indicating

on the one hand you couldn't win without money but on the other saying it was possible if you had the right players. When I brought this up to Sky and Whitman, they seemed disinterested in the observation. They were impressed with Karlov's vast storehouse of knowledge, and they wanted to draw on it at a later date to help with fielding the right personnel.

At this point in the journey, I still hadn't much enthusiasm for the program. My motivation for even appearing to care was that I didn't want to disappoint Sky, nor did I want to have her think less of me as a maturing man. The reality was, however, that I simply had no lust for any aspect of baseball.

To my surprise, Whitman seemed to be gravitating more toward Sky's position, at least in so far as he was sensing a challenge that was alluring. Often I'd notice him deep in contemplation and when I'd ask him what it was, he'd respond that he believed as Sky did that we were missing some special ingredient that would allow us to do what had never before been accomplished.

He admitted he had no idea what it might be but I could see it was irking him that he didn't.

CHAPTER 9: SPRING TRAINING

It was hard to believe but we were about to enter our first, and no doubt last, spring training. Sky was in her glory, the happiest I'd ever seen her. Most of her time was spent digesting every conceivable fact she could about baseball. She was a speed-reader and had a remarkable power of memory. She was getting to where she could rattle off statistics while conversing with the likes of a guy as knowledgeable as Karlov. In fact, not infrequently she'd call on him to discuss one decision or another, developing a working relationship with the professor.

All of the players that were eligible for free agency, or had no commitment to our club, had left. We were also able to dispose of the richer contract players and thus had a couple bucks to pick up a few second-rate pitchers and batters. No matter how she maneuvered, however, it was still at best a rag-tag collection of men on our roster.

It peeved her knowing that the team we had at the time would never be able to win the bet she'd made with Thorne. Plus, I could tell it pressured her that she was responsible for a wager that had a high probability of setting the team back for the following several years. Frequently she'd resort to expletives to express her frustration. That was typically followed by statements that I surmised were no more than blind optimism; generally she'd declare that the three of us were brilliant enough to see what none before us had been able to glean and thus in the end, we'd prevail.

I played the role I believed she wanted to see me in, sympathizing with her consternation and reinforcing her wild cheerfulness. What I never did was step up to the romance plate, not even to bring up the subject of a date.

One afternoon we were on the field observing the team working out. Sky was interested in every aspect of the operation of the team, including how the players were being prepared physically, mentally and spiritually for the opening of the season.

On this occasion, she was watching the pitchers warming up. I was standing next to her when I noticed one of our men racing in the outfield to catch a deep fly. As he approached the ball, he made a leaping grab, catching the ball but coming down in an awkward manner, his right foot twisting in such a way that his whole body came crashing to the ground.

Immediately some of the players and coaches were running to his aid; he wasn't moving. We walked over to have a look. He was laying in agony, clutching his right knee. The pain must have been extraordinary because the player, Figgie Reese, one of our new outfielder prospects, was near tears by the time the physical therapist arrived.

After inspecting the leg for only a brief time, Max Barber, the therapist, was overheard calling for a stretcher. Figgie was carried away. Barber came over to Sky and myself.

"I'm sorry. I'm sure this is not what you want to hear but there's serious internal damage. He'll need surgery for certain and I'd guess it's the end of the year for him."

"I had high hopes for Reese. He's a guy who was dying for a chance and I believe he could have really produced for us," Sky lamented. She took several steps, making a large circle before finally ending up where she began. "Just what we needed," she groaned.

"It's only our first injury," I consoled her.

"We can't afford a first. Where's Whitman?" she barked irritably.

"In the office. He's running numbers; researching loser players some of the teams want to dump, and some minor leaguers as well."

"Ben, would you mind telling him to focus on

outfielders who can catch a f-in ball without tripping over themselves?" She stomped off fitfully—the happy-go-lucky girl she had been in the past was now displaying temperament fits.

Before I could take off on the assignment, Flip Montil exited the dugout and was following a line straight toward us. He started blabbering at us before he reached where we were standing.

"My agent said he's tried to reach you several times to work out my trade but you don't return his calls. Come on now, several teams want me and you guys can get a great deal out of it."

Flip was the consummate power ball player. He was just over six foot tall and built like a rock. His brown hair was straight as it aimed for the shoulders but then just as it was about to land it appeared to have a change of heart and flipped upward minutely at the ends—it parted naturally on the left. His thick eyebrows were color-coordinated as was the short-cropped goatee, the latter accentuating his small round lips.

His eye slits were perpetually worn with a narrow spacing, memorializing him in a pose battling the sun's rays to catch a fly ball. Flip Montil strutted as if vanity was a birthright. He was without a doubt the man's man, a perfect copy of the actor Brad Pitt—I detested his swaggering conceit before this tale commenced and despised him worse as it unfolded.

"All I'm asking for is a trade," he sighed intentionally

at Sky. "I don't want the best years of my career wasted like this."

"Can't do it right now, buddy," I stepped in, relishing in the pleasure of serving him defeat.

"I'm worth a bundle," he appealed toward Sky, ignoring me entirely.

"We need you," Sky answered. "Hell, you're still making a respectable salary."

"That's true but money isn't the only thing I care about."

As we were talking, an errant ball rolled in our direction. One of the players came to pick it up. He motioned for me to come and talk with him, which I did; this left Sky and Flip to haggle over his contract.

"What else is it you're here for besides the money?" Sky posed to him.

"It's very simple. I'd like to have a few more shots at post-season play. I'd miss it. Let's be honest, there's no way it's happening here."

"What if we work together to make it happen? Right here with this new, young team?"

"I have no confidence in that." Flip momentarily switched his focus. He looked down on Sky's much smaller frame, using his allure as a weapon to capture her in his visual grip. "This team does have one bit of appeal...they have the cutest GM I've ever seen. You may rouse my interest in pre-season play, regular-season play, and a few other kinds of play too." Then he unloaded a single barrel of his charm gun, an enchantment bullet ordered to sweep her into his arms. "Wow! I could lose my focus, yes I could, my little boss."

"I heard you're the all-around player," Sky coquettishly hurled back at him.

"I have that reputation. So, what do you think about finding out?"

"What I want to find out is what it's going to take to get you to put out a hundred percent for us. Flip we need you."

"And what are you putting out for me," he questioned provocatively.

"All immediate hope of being traded. Douse your bat on that," she said playfully.

"Well, well. Look how nice we're getting along already. You and I may just be a thing; one of those works-in-progress."

As Flip was coming on to Sky, nodding his head so she wouldn't mistake his reaction as anything other than inspiration, Whitman came out of the dugout. He walked in my direction and at the same time called out for Sky to join us.

Sky was still cleverly toying with Flip; she was fully aware he was doing the same with her. Flip was in the mood for play. He picked up a glove and tossed it to Sky but she dropped it.

"Try throwing the ball during your business meetings;

get the real feel of the game, you know?" Flip smiled as he ran off.

By this time, Whitman and I had joined Sky. She picked up two other gloves and handed one each to Whitman and me.

"Let's talk," she said, inviting Whitman to continue.

"What's this for?" I asked while pointing to the glove I now had on my left hand.

"Come on, guys. Let's at least play a little catch while we talk, get a better feeling for what our players are doing," she suggested.

Whitman seemed impatient, as if he had something to say and limited tolerance for Sky's antics. Still, she spread us out so that there was several feet distance between us. Then she took the ball she had in her glove and attempted to hurl it at me. Her whole body rotated clumsily, the side-arm-thrown ball flew randomly far from me. I ran to retrieve it and then tested my arm by aiming it at Whitman. As I did, the torque to my body from the faulty mechanics caused the muscles in my shoulder to tweak. I laughed at myself.

Sky was insistent that we try to hone our skills. We humored her for several minutes before it became obvious to her that we indeed did suck; not one ball was caught before Whitman ran out of tolerance—how the guy starred at wresting I couldn't imagine except that his power was so exceptional and his fearsomeness so remarkable that he terrified the competition; it couldn't have been his fine motor control.

"Sky, Ben, for Christ sakes we need to talk," he blurted out.

There was urgency in his voice, a tonal quality I'd only heard from him on a couple occasions, both when he perceived he had made an amazing intellectual breakthrough.

"Remember in the bar when I first introduced you both to Karlov and I said I was thinking about an idea?" His excitement was indomitable.

"Not really, but what's the point," Sky answered.

"Maybe, I never even expressed it. Anyways, I totally lost what I was thinking. That never happens when I'm on to something. For a long time, it was out of my consciousness. Then all of a sudden a few weeks ago, there it was. I never said anything to either of you because I wasn't sure it would go anywhere. Then I started looking into—"

"Whitman, you tease. Just get to the point," Sky admonished.

"The bear during our orientation week. It was a miracle that we all weren't killed, right?"

"And we'll need another miracle to win with this team. That's a huge breakthrough, Whitman," I kidded him.

"No way. I'm not talking about miracles. I'm talking about us, the three of us together. That's what happened.

Ben had the grace to absorb the powerful impact by the animal, I used what I knew about body mechanics to counter his force, and Sky calculated the precise location to strike a life-saving blow."

"Okay, so we were all contributing something. I don't get what all the excitement is about," Sky said, directing her thought my way.

"Just slow down. I promise this will be worth it. So what I was wondering was what might it be that the three of us could bring to the game that nobody else has."

"Oh, I got it," I continued making fun of him. "Since I'll probably be a composer, I'll write symphonies to swoon this bunch of nobodies into The World Series."

"You hit it, Beethoven."

"I'm not *that* good. Remember, no miracles."

"With our help, you might be good enough," Whitman professed earnestly.

"Well, now that you've thoroughly confused us, and aroused our curiosity, I suppose we're going to have to wade through one of your endless lectures before we get the answer?" she poked away at him.

"It is going to be a long one. In fact, I've been preoccupied with this since it came to me the second time. Okay, let me start here. I'll give you the summary first. We're going to use sound as it's never been used before in any sport. Ben will compose the music, Sky, you'll do the mathematical analysis and impact studies, and I'll do the neurological programs. When our players hear the sounds we're going to subject them to, they're going to play better."

"But we already went over this; that's yesterday's news," Sky said dismissively. "Every team and player—"

"That's infant level stuff they're doing with music and enhanced performance. We're going way beyond that realm, into a space where nobody has gone before."

"Lost me, Whit, but what else is new?" I quipped.

"Remember a couple weeks ago, I said I had to leave to see my uncle? It was true that I flew to Miami to be with him but the reason I went was not because of a family gathering," Whitman admitted. "What I wanted to discuss with him I didn't' believe wise to do on the phone or through email. His response assured me that my judgment was correct.

"Here's the story. My uncle used to work for the government. He's a neurological researcher and was last employed by an agency called DARPA, the Defense Advanced Research Projects Agency. Specifically, he was assigned to what they call a Neural Prostheses Program."

"Sounds fairly benign to me," Sky commented. "What's the big whoop?"

"If you call the capability of controlling the thoughts and emotions of literally every human being on earth benign, then I guess it's not a big deal. But the technology exists to do it, and in some instances it's been used already to influence specific groups of people—I'll be giving you all the research and you can both check it out for yourselves to see if it's not valid.

"There's a patent that was issued to a man named Lowery that goes back to 1992. At the time, he called his project the *Silent Subliminal Presentation System*. Let me summarize the abstract for the patent: It's a silent communication system that couples extreme sound amplitudes and frequencies with a desired intelligence in such a way that through acoustics and vibration you can feed the brain messages that control the emotional productions of the mind. This application can be achieved through transducers, earphones or loudspeakers...and get this, you can even store the material and reuse it over and over."

"Sounds like science fiction to me," Sky said, rubbing her eyes.

"It's not at all. That's the shocking part of it. It's been used, I know it."

"How can you be sure?" I asked.

"Well, first, my uncle never responded to the question of whether or not the reports on its use were true. Instead he told me that his involvement with any government-related work he did was classified. But then when I posed a hypothetical to him about how I thought I might use music to improve a person's ability to learn, or even to deliver low frequency messages, like subliminal cuts, he nodded and smiled. Then he told me it was 'definitely' a line of inquiry I should pursue.

"So you went further with it, I suppose?" Sky prompted him to go on.

"Of course. It's amazing what's been done, though the government wouldn't admit any of it. Look, I'll keep this simple. Let's say a person is experiencing a certain emotion, like extreme fear. Scientists are able to identify the concomitant brainwave patterns. Now, if they can duplicate them then they can place those same clusters on what they call the Silent Cloud carrier frequencies. From there, they can silently trigger the same emotional reaction in any human that is first targeted and second subjected to the Cloud material.

"The brain has no conscious awareness of what is happening to cause the affect and, therefore, no ability whatsoever to defend against it. The positive applications being researched are amazing, from methods of relaxation and meditation to treating psychosomatic illness to trying to remediate deafness.

"On the other side of the spectrum is where the evil uses come in. It's more than a rumor that this technology was experimented with successfully by America in a foreign country during wartime. It accounted for an unprecedented number of surrenders by troops that hadn't even fought: there were documented instances where soldiers were giving up in droves. They used this technology to literally enter the brains of these soldiers, manipulate their electroencephalograph (EEG) patterns, and thus disable them by injecting, as if with a syringe, terrifying emotional feeling states."

"Okay, so what does this have to do with us? We're not the U.S. military and we don't have the equipment to do this. Plus, would we want to? Hell, Whitman, we'd surely be breaking the law if we tried, at least violating their patent," Sky calculated.

"Sky, first we'd only be using it to do good. Secondly, I've already figured out a way to accomplish the same outcome and more but without infringing on their patent," Whitman proudly announced. "This is benign. All we're doing is playing music. The low frequency patterns we'll interject that the brain will never be able to detect are going to relax, arouse or stimulate our men… it'll make them better players. Darling, I'm just trying to bring you your wish."

"Whitman you're out of your mind—that's an established fact. All I'm concerned about is not getting imprisoned or violating ethical or moral standards."

"You won't be, I promise. I'll show you everything we do each step of the way. All I need from you is the mathematical models and analysis, and from Ben here, the sounds that will camouflage the hidden codes that will elicit the proper brain patterns we're looking for.

"This is actually no different from what is being done daily by hundreds of businesses that attempt to use various forms of subtle advertisements to promote their products. We're going to take meditation and enhancement techniques to a new level of effectiveness," Whitman concluded.

"What do you think, Ben?" Sky asked me.

"You just have to tell me what sorts of music you want."

"We'll have some pieces we use for the whole team, like during practices or in the gym. Then the players can have their own sounds that they use when working out or preparing for the game," Whitman explained. "But first we need to test this out and see if we can deliver the goods."

"Music. Baseball. What the hell," Sky celebrated.

As she was expressing her enthusiasm, Flip lunged past where we were. He finally reached the ball he'd been chasing. As he did he stopped to insert a comment.

"You three are the sorriest excuse for athletes I've ever seen," he chuckled as he watched us continue dropping the balls we were still tossing back and forth.

"What are you talking about?" we retorted in unison, laughing because we all knew the statement was true.

CHAPTER 10: MAKING IT WORK

Whitman dove head first into the project. I assumed that his motivation was purely scientific. Had I thought about it more carefully I would have recognized that there was far more at stake for him than either the intellectual challenge or the success of the team, or both.

Sky was more transparent. She was determined to prove herself worthy of running an organization. She reasoned that executives managing every team sought an edge over their competition. If Whitman's approach was doable, she planned to employ it to its fullest potential. This was especially the case after Whitman showed her the data supporting him veering around the prior patent and being able to deliver the hidden brain instructions in an even more effective manner than had been done previously.

I was tickled. After everything that had transpired, I was being called upon to do what I loved most, create music. In fact, it was Sky who returned my violin that she had hidden away from me in her closet.

Within a couple weeks of Whitman making his proposal, our apartment must have looked similar to the data center for the Atomic Energy Commission. Not only were there my instruments and recording equipment, but Whitman had also scattered around the room innumerable computers with monitors where he and Sky worked feverishly.

I'm certain had any of our parents visited they would have been appalled. The remnants of food and drink were everywhere, a mass of clutter and mess that contradicted our typical respect for cleanliness.

I recall one morning composing a new sound for one of the players, at the same time noticing Whitman sitting in front of one of his computer monitors. He was positioned such that his right foot was under his left buttock and he was inclined forward, his head so close to the screen that he had to be damaging his eyes—he was intense any time he used his mind.

Then all of a sudden, the monitor started flashing bright colors and patterns of light, one after another in rapid succession, along with an annoying beeping sound.

"Ben, take a look," Whitman shouted. "See those explosions, all the lights and colors? That's the precise

EEG pattern of the brain when in a state of high energy. Now watch this," he instructed as he fiddled with his keyboard. In an instant, the brightness faded to dull colorations and the designs moved slowly rather than at high speed across the screen. "That's deep meditation... identical for all humans. If I could deliver this in a subliminal form this minute, I would have you as unthinking as a guru in prayer."

Whitman then tapped a few notes on his keyboard, mumbling gaily, "Cool."

"I'd say it is. So it all works?"

"Ben, this is just the beginning. The real challenge is going to be first to deliver the clusters that feed the brain with the desired states and then to test their effectiveness. I'm counting on Sky coming through with the experimental models that we'll use to test this baby."

"It still seems eerie to me. I mean, getting inside another person's brain and with them not knowing that it's happening," I squinted.

"We're all nothing but tiny neural machines. All we're doing is tinkering with what's already been programmed into us through millions of years of evolution. We're on the side of good here," Whitman proclaimed, appointing us ambassadors on the high road of morality. "What we need to be concerned about is what our government is up to. You can be sure that they're capable of putting all of us into any condition or emotion they wish, and keeping us there without disclosing what they're doing."

"Wow."

What Whitman was explaining overwhelmed me. I didn't know whether or not to believe him, but I certainly wished he were wrong.

"This could be big, Ben. We're going to stimulate cerebral progressions and then exploit them like it's never been done."

Whitman went back to this keyboard, again using his fingers to create a rhythm, a distinct rapid burst of taps suggestive of approbation for what he was accomplishing.

It would be well over a week before the next key event occurred.

The setting was the same. Whitman and I were home working on the project. Sky was out and about. This time, however, after a brief period, Sky burst through the front door.

"Did it come through yet?" she questioned as she approached one of the screens; at the same time a printer began rapidly spitting out pages. "Let's see if this stuff really works," she mused while examining one sheet after another. "It's un-b-f-in-lievable," she exclaimed enthusiastically. "Thank god. Maybe we'll be able to clean this place up soon."

"Come on, Sky. Let's hear the details," Whitman requested.

"Try this for starters, Whit. I used six players in the experimental group. We measured their batting with their normal music, no music and our music. The statistical difference between no music and their choice of sound was insignificant. On the other hand, our music resulted in an over twenty percent improvement above either of the other two conditions," she reported. "I'll do some trial runs with the pitchers tomorrow if you can have everything ready for me, Whit."

"Should we call it Magic Music?" I wondered out loud.

"Call it what you want. To me, we have created winning music," Sky retorted.

"This is the type of application of science that changes peoples' lives," Whitman asserted. "You both realize what we've done."

"Sure, we're playing baseball the old fashioned way— win any way you can," Sky smirked.

"I guess it's time for a celebration," I interjected. "Here, try my new sound. We can use it for background."

The actress Sky jumped up on the table in the middle of them room, hollering as if she were trying to be heard over the impassioned crowd at Ripley's.

"Tell me if I ain't sane but I'd say things may change. We're headed for glory and I can't wait to let the celebration rain. Tell me if I ain't right but I think we're eyeing delight. Guys, I think it's time for music and I wanna sing. And it's a time for stupid childish things. Let's smile a while like kings and dance 'til silence screams."

Sky then yielded to Whit. "We found a pot of gold, so

let the moment take its hold. Bold men may lose their souls but we'll be dancing 'til our fans are old." Whitman paused to be certain our attention was complete. "And it wasn't even too complex," he exulted, "just looked at the insular frontal cortex; it was sitting there in the precise locale, of the ventromedial vesticular canal.

"What!?" Sky and I chuckled as Whit's neuro-lingo floated over our heads. "Well, whatever. The point is…" Sky finished up, "that we got it right and things are already looking bright. We're headed for fortune and fame and I can't wait to let the celebration rain."

By now we were all dancing around the room. Indeed, we were in a festive mood, sharing the thrill of success together. What was better was that each of us had a different cause for rejoicing.

CHAPTER 11: BETTER THAN DRUGS

By the time opening day arrived, our players were ecstatic. Most of them were young, unproven in the majors up to that point in their careers, or with little or no big league experience. They were the castoffs and leftovers, the players that had been categorized by every other team in the down-and-going rather than up-and-coming grouping. Yet, here they were composing the members of the once mighty Blue Stripes. More astonishing, especially to them, was that they were singularly improving beyond their imagination, and together as a group congealing into a strong unit.

How the players conceptualized the unbelievable status of the team was of no consequence to us, but in overhearing their discussions, they generally veered toward a scientific-philosophic position, positing that there are indeed occasions when the whole is far greater than the sum of the pieces composing it. What that outlook did for the boys was bond them together in such a way that they couldn't imagine playing without one another—the unintended consequence of our music, which we had strategically and diligently introduced into their routine, was that our boys were as closely united as any team could be.

One of the only players left over from the Thorne-era was Flip, and even he was gaga over his performance. By the time he was in the clubhouse getting ready for the first game of the year, he was flying on a magic carpet, his new mates sitting at his feet.

In the locker room that eventful day there was music permeating the space. Nobody paid any attention to it, with the exception of Whitman, Sky and I. We were being as inconspicuous as possible while furtively glancing gloriously at our players. Flip was the leader of the team, the only player making a respectable major league salary and the one they all rallied around for advice and infusions of confidence.

We watched as Flip flitted into the room, gaily taking a few dance steps before grabbing a couple of his team mates by the arm and engaging them as partners, spinning them around in a circle a few times, and then loosening his grip. Next, he tapped his way over to another player, Stretch, a pitcher we picked up on the cheap from Baltimore's farm system; he was reported to have an arm so worn out that as a player he had less prospect than a typewriter salesman.

Flip reached out his hand toward Stretch, an obvious display of tease in that he made a theatrical routine out of the gesture, moving his extremity ever so slowly before comically poking Stretch as if he were a wicked witch goading him with an pitchfork. Stretch's face showed angst, not due to the dramatics but rather to the physical act of being touched. Quickly, and without ceremony, he returned the tactile gesture. Flip was hysterical.

"I almost forgot about your little worry," Flip taunted with a giant smile.

The shocking part of the story was that Stretch, exceeding his potential by light years during spring training, was on schedule to open the season for us. How did our opening day pitcher handle luck? He refused to let anyone touch him on the day he pitched, without him touching back in return. (As an aside, once when I was talking with him on an afternoon he was due to pitch I asked him how long he had practiced the ritual regarding being touched. He proudly informed me that it had been his quirky habit since high school. I nodded my head while wondering to myself what on earth possessed him to embrace this loony ritual all those years, all the time flopping shamefully as a pitcher.)

"You got me back, didn't you, Stretch?" Flip clowned before shaking his head in disbelief, the gesture altering his facial expression to one of mystification. "Where do you guys come up with these wild ideas?"

Flip didn't wait for an answer, his elation at the moment propelling him to whirl from player to player, touching each of them to emphasize his mock of Stretch.

"Listen to that sound," I tried whispering to Whitman who was standing next to me. My excitement overmastered heed; my words flowed at a greater volume than was wise. "Nobody would believe what it can do."

"Shush," Whitman giddily cautioned me. "I think it works."

"They still have to win games," Sky giggled, unable to defeat the urge for a public celebration of our great achievement. "My god," she cried out as she pulled Whitman and me into a huddle. "It's working on us; can't you tell?"

"I'll turn the volume down," I offered.

"Ben," she sneered. "Don't be a killjoy."

We settled each other down and continued watching the show. Our new leadoff hitter, a guy squinting in the mirror forty years of age, and about to tackle the last season of his career, Gus, approached Flip.

"My Lord, man, I've never seen you so trippy. What's hyping you up?"

"No idea. But you can see what's been going on since we started training. All I can figure is that the break was rejuvenating." He stopped to admire his fine physique. "I just feel swell. I can't wait to get out there."

156

The music I had created for our project varied from jazz to rock to rhythm and blues to hip-hop beats to ballads. Each piece had been infused with the subliminal brain messages we determined would stimulate the players. We varied the presentation of sound in a purposeful order. As Flip was talking with Gus, a new song began, setting Flip into a singing mood. During the festivities he led his troop to dance around the seats and lockers, the players with bats in hand, spinning joyfully.

"I got this warming feeling; I got this little flame. I'm in the dandiest mood boys; I'm in the mood for a ballgame. Does anyone have the same peachy feeling? Who feels this feelin' I'm feelin' that pulling me out to the field?"

Flip ran over to our skinny utility infielder, Umberto Rojas, a good-humored kid who could hardly speak English. "I have some lines for you, Umberto. I'll whisper them to you…then you give it a whirl."

In broken English, our player from Mexico gave it his best shot. "I know we're odds on losers, sure to miss the biggest spreads. We'll probably fall to the bottom and quickly lose our confidence. But something crazy tells me I'm in for a batting spree and all the slander in the world just couldn't get to me."

Flip patted him on the shoulder as a reward for a fine effort. He then continued with more lines. "I know I've doubted this team. I said we'd fall in shame. I've talked my trash about it and a few of you have done the same.

157

But something seems real right now; something seems to fit. There's something in my gut now, and I like the feeling kids."

Flip led the way as the whole team put the finishing touches on the piece.

"We're all a-buzz and there's a flood of passion pouring in our veins. What a rise; perhaps the skies showered luck on us today. The summer's season's come to be and we're all ready for the job. So go and doubt us…but something about us…might just leave you in awe."

When the song ended each of the players gathered around, with Flip in the center of the room. They all clasped one another, a giant collective bear hug. Then they formed a long line, Stretch walking along it and touching every player one time.

"It's opening day!" they all yelled out together after Stretch completed his routine.

The players then did their last minute preparations, grabbing gear, pounding gloves, blackening bats, tightening belts and pulling up socks. I noticed one of our fellows smelling what looked to me like a dead fish, which he then placed daintily in his locker. Another juggled three balls and yet another crossed his heart.

"To Flip's right," Cary Collins, a relief pitcher, commented to a player standing next to him. "This team's new and young but we have something special."

"A bunch of nobodies we are," Danny Gomez chuckled.

"Somebody forgot to tell us," Cary answered.

I overheard their conversation and so did my father. He'd arrived a few minutes earlier but had likely been brain altered as by the music, like the rest of us. He was in the grandest of mood. He moved close to where we were standing, inspecting each of us in turn several times before addressing us collectively.

"You kids are up to something," he smirked. "I can smell it," he sniffed with an amused grin of non-belief. He started to walk away but couldn't resist a warning. "Just avoid lawsuits; they're an expensive mess."

CHAPTER 12: THE SEASON GOES ON

Time moves quickly when you're having fun. I understood the goal was to turn a profit but for me the joy was watching Sky. She ate, slept, dreamed and drank baseball. Sure, we were winning. We had a secret weapon that none of our competition could have imagined us possessing. Even so, it seemed to mean nothing to Sky in terms of her attitude toward her job. She believed we could still lose and because of that she was increasingly more dedicated to her role—she was becoming a star as a businessperson.

Indeed, the other GMs either ignored her or despised her, and the other management personnel working for our team no doubt resented her but knew better than to challenge her. Still, each and every one of them was aware that she was the leader of the three of us when it came to making decisions for the "organization," the term she delighted used to embellish The Blue Stripes "brand."

She was also developing a relationship with my father. I could see he admired her yet surprisingly I never sensed he resented or judged me for not being the one handling the affairs of business rather than she. It was an event that had taken place very early in the season that had deepened the connection between Sky and Arnold Wolf.

The afternoon game had ended. Most of the fans were on their way to their cars. Darrin North had taken his son, nine year-old Tommie, to the ballpark. Mr. North was a blue-collar worker who had saved for two weeks to have the money for the game. They'd sat in the bleachers and shared a great time, The Blue Stripes slaughtering of all teams, Thorne's Rivals.

Young Tommie needed to use the bathroom before they left and thus by the time they ventured to their car, most of the crowd had disbursed. There were a few scattered people in the parking lot with Mr. North and his boy. However, when interviewed, none who witnessed the tragedy were able to explain what the father could have done to provoke two hoodlums who must have boozed excessively during the game to assault him.

North was a frail, spindly man. The prevailing opinion of those who saw what happened likened it to a weak schoolboy catching the eye of a bully. At first, the twosome began teasing and taunting the father. Then as he ignored them, it incited them to rage. Finally, North shouted for them to back off, pleading that he was with his son and didn't want trouble.

His plea was ignored. In fact, the confrontation turned physical. Eventually, the two men began beating on North, so savagely that when they were finished he was lying still on the pavement. The two walked off smugly, laughing like pranksters.

They had no vehicle and were never found.

The little boy fell to the ground to revive his father. Within minutes—too many of them—a security officer came to the scene and called for an ambulance. It should have been a hearse. Mr. North had been kicked in the head and developed a massive bleed, dying during the precious minutes before help arrived.

My father wept.

He blamed himself for the horror of that evening in spite of the fact that he had a security team that exceeded that of any other professional sport franchise. There was nothing he could do to remedy the hurt for the innocent surviving family.

My father wept.

As expected, Mrs. North filed a lawsuit and the matter was headline news. The media loved to demonize my father from the start of his ownership of the team. Rumors were floating when he bought The Blue Stripes that the owner of the leading newspaper and several radio and television channels had wanted to make the purchase but was outfoxed by my father who convinced the seller that the team would be a better franchise under his ownership.

Needless to say, the North matter was better than feeding candy to a child. They smeared him every inch of the way. My father ignored them. His concern was the North family. The man asked the attorney representing them what his demand was: when he answered my father told him it was too little. The suit was dropped and settled out of court.

A trust was established with enough money to provide income for Mrs. North and her family for the rest of her life. When she died, the funds in the trust would revert to young Tommie. Then after the matter was completed, my father went further, usurping for the first time the authority of his three GMs by making an offer to Tommie to become a team batboy.

Despite the public upbraiding by the press, the old man cared nothing except for the heartbreak of these people—he never attempted to defend himself, ignoring the advice of his PR people. Refusing to disclose the terms of the settlement were the only conditions he placed on the North family.

As hard-ass as he could be, he had a heart as big as a country. Due to the fact that the calamity took place under our tenure, Sky, Whitman and I had to know what transpired. Sky couldn't get over how he handled the affair; she nearly revered my father, not only due to his compassion but also because of his brashness. She watched diligently how he dealt with conflicts and challenges; she behaved like the understudy he no doubt had hoped I would be.

We were about at the half way mark in the season and winning our way to respectability in the league. I recall it was after one of the games close to this point in the season, when we were all in the locker room after a game. The players had been shuffling in, dirty uniforms and lots of fresh smiles. I watched as Tommie North ran up to Flip to take his batting glove from him.

"Anything else I can do for you, Flip?" Tommie asked.

Flip grabbed the boy by the shoulders and drew him in for a hug.

"Best damn batboy in the whole league, guaranteed," Flip smiled as he grasped the boy a second time.

My father had just walked in, accompanied by a distinguished looking man I recognized as the new Mayor Tollini.

"Tommie," my dad called out, "come over here. I want to introduce you to Mayor Tollini."

Tommie stretched out his little arm as straight as the bat he was toting in his other hand.

"Good to meet you, sir."

"You too, son. Your team is tearing up the league," Tollini complimented as if Tommie were the manager.

"We're going all the way this year," Tommie promised.

"Well, you got yourself one hell of a start."

Tollini dismissed the boy with a tender shove on the shoulder, Tommie dashing off to high-five a few of the players.

"That's the son of the man killed here at the park," my dad informed him. Then he fudged on the details of how Tommie became the team mascot. "My son and his friends chose him to be batboy."

"Nice touch," Tollini complimented. Then as he stared across the room he couldn't help asking my father about what he was observing. "What are they doing?"

The players were lining up to march by Amos Hoskins, our back-up catcher. As they passed, Amos dispensed a wisp of dusty material on their arm. The procession was interrupted, however, when a sport commentator, Monty Pick, accompanied by his camera-man, approached them.

Flip was nearby and Pick called him over.

"Another great game for The Blue Stripes," Pick mentioned before praising Flip. "Another great one for you too, Flip. What is that, seven home runs in your last eight games? Your team is leading the division. I don't need to tell you there's a lot of speculation how you guys are doing so well. Can you enlighten us?"

Pick now waved toward Amos, as curious as The Mayor as to what the players were doing.

"I can't explain it; some voodoo secret Hoskins

believes is warding off any lurking evil spirits intent on ending our run," Flip snickered.

"Everyone said it would take a miracle to turn this team around. Maybe you fellows found one," Pick voiced into his microphone.

"As long as we're winning, every last man can believe whatever gives them inspiration," Flip jeered as he eyed the men who were still parading past Amos.

Pick began moving toward where Amos was apportioning his magic brew.

"Maybe I should sample some of that," he called out to Amos.

"Only for team members," Amos chastened him.

"Well, can you at least tell us something about it?"

"It's from a Gypsy Lady. That's all I know," Amos answered into the microphone.

Flip had been interviewed by Pick many times in the past and was in the mood for a prank. He approached the commentator from behind with a bottle of water and poured it on his head. After doing so, he wrapped his arm around Pick's waist, smiling devilishly into the camera.

"Monty, it's all about having a good time; that's our secret to success," Flip playfully informed him.

"That may be all it takes to foster a winning team," Pick announced to his audience, wiping the water off his forehead, "players having a good time. From KCAB this is Monty Pick inside The Blue Stripes locker room."

Pick was still drying himself when he whispered to his cameraman. "We off, Larry?"

As soon as the man signaled affirmatively, Pick grabbed up a cup of water and started chasing after Flip. "Damn it, Flip, you're paying to have my suit cleaned."

Pick nearly crashed into my father, who was still observing the scene with Tollini.

"They're serious about this Gypsy Lady business?" Tollini asked in a perplexed tone.

"There's no sport like baseball when it comes to superstitions. These players believe that a broken bat or bad bounce can cost them a game, even a year's work can come to disaster over one random mishap. So, whatever is working when they're winning, they keep doing it," my dad answered.

Most of the players had received their ration of the pixie dust and were disbursing to their lockers. Sky, Whitman and I were joking with our players, dispensing back slaps and handshakes for a job well done.

"Dad, what do you think?" I called out, having not discussed the progress of the team directly with him for a few weeks.

My dad dismissed himself from Tollini and came over to where I was standing.

"I hope these fellows don't dive into a slump," he whispered to me.

"It's not going to happen," Whitman answered him, overhearing my dad.

"You kids…you're still not going to tell me what you're doing, are you? Oh, I know a thing or two, enough to know something fishy is happening."

"Dad, we're succeeding. Isn't that what you wanted?" I posed.

"Winning baseball games is not success, it is fun. When you discover success, you'll know what I mean. And trust me, I want you to have it."

It was the weirdest exchange. We looked into each other's eyes; I'll swear it was a moment of pure aware-ness of one another. I understood that for Arnold Wolf there could never be any other definition of success but making a buck. He might win The World Series but would still be peeved if it happened with a money losing team.

Yet at that instant I believe he knew he had been par-roting words for years to me that were true to his world view but not mine. It was at that instant, in my opinion, that he had forsaken his wish to mold me into a second coming of him.

CHAPTER 13: BEHIND CLOSED DOORS

We each had our own office, although I'd estimate that Sky spent triple the time in hers that Whitman and I together spent in ours. Generally, she'd arrive for work stylishly attired, in one of the many business outfits she'd purchased. She had her hair blown out weekly.

I used to droll over her in the past when I'd see her on campus in a pair of Levi's blue jeans and a red sweatshirt with her pink tennis shoes that she loved accenting with green laces. Then lounging around our apartment she'd wear her flannel PJ's with the cutest oversized furry slippers. I honestly couldn't have imagined her looking better.

At first when she assumed the executive image I balked, but I never expressed my disappointment. I

came to realize that I was threatened, Sky moving eagerly into a man's world that felt as foreign to me as a jock
strap. Once I made that admission to myself, it seemed
to change my perception. Then I was able to appreciate
the beauty she possessed as a more glamorous figure;
if anything, her sensuality piqued my appetite all the
more.

I had caught sight of her coming in one morning
while I was making my way down the hall toward the
lunchroom to get a cup of coffee. There was no real purpose being at the office other than as a show of support
for her; we both knew it but pretended otherwise. After
mixing my cream and sugar, I proceeded to my office.

Sky had gone into hers. By the time I passed, she had
shut the door. Had I been able to voyeur on her I would
have observed her in a high spirits. She was applying
makeup in front of a mirror and then she ran her fingers
through her soft hair. Her neck was long and slender,
partially draping her straight falling hairdo.

She examined herself and then twirled around the
office. Finally, she went to the fax machine and took out
the several sheets of paper resting in the tray, dropping
them heedlessly on her desk.

"Sky here," she responded to the ringing phone,
pausing to listen to the message of the caller. "The trade
deadline is still weeks away but I'll get back to you soon
Mr. Grisham.

After hanging up, she continued experiencing her

joyous state, frolicking through the office until startled by a knock on her door. She rushed to her desk, sitting down to assume a more formal pose before addressing whomever was coming to see her.

"Come in," she finally called out.

The door opened. There was Flip, standing holding a stunning bouquet of bright red roses mixed with white Casa Blanca lilies. He entered, closing the door behind him. Holding the flowers in his right hand, he reached out to offer them to Sky.

"These are for you," he smiled.

"You don't believe in making appointments," she chided.

"This isn't an appointment," he countered, still holding out the flowers.

Sky finally took the gift, laying it across her desktop.

"Well, thank you. Now, Flip, what can I do for you?"

"May I be candid?" Flip posed to her.

"Only if I don't have to listen," Sky retorted flippantly.

It was during the beginning of the exchange that I happened past her office. Well, my phrasing might suggest it was by chance that I was near her workspace but the truth was that on my way back to my office, I was fishing for an excuse to visit with her—the amazing thing was that we lived together but with the team dominating her life I rarely saw her, let alone have time to hang out together.

I had made up the dumb pretense of wanting to

discuss a new song I was working on. Regardless, as I approached her door I heard voices. I thought I vaguely recognized the male sound but couldn't place it. Thus, I put my ear to the door and listened, never considering the strong likelihood that someone would pass by and wonder what I was doing spying on my associate.

"Do you know where my name comes from?"

The moment I heard his words, I knew it was Flip speaking. My first reaction was to take offense to him being alone behind closed doors with her.

"I'd hope your parents weren't so cruel to choose the name, Flip," Sky teased.

"They're not that bad but they did name me Xavier. I'm not sure what they were thinking. It never mattered because as far back as grade school everyone saw me as a light-hearted, almost frivolous, soul. One day in class in the second or third grade, my teacher asked me a question and I answered. She started laughing. 'Xavier,' she said to me, 'you are a flippant one.' One of my classmates asked what the word meant and she sent us all to the dictionary with an assignment. From that day, I became Flip, the flippant one, to all my friends."

"It fits," Sky agreed. "You are always—"

"Light…when everyone else seems so serious?"

"You said it perfectly," Sky commended him.

The exchange was too informal for my taste. I kept my ear glued to the door.

"That's what I bring to the world, my little manager.

But there is more to me." Flip used a pause and discerning stare to secure her attention. "Look, Sky, I don't always have the perfect words to express myself."

"A not uncommon affliction for males, I promise you."

"What I'm saying is I have fun being around you; and if I'm not mistaken you don't exactly hate hanging with me."

"Flip, we're in the middle of the season, I'm your boss, and—"

"Doesn't matter to me. I've been thinking about you. Sure, you're the modern day business woman but there's a lot more I've figured out."

The room went silent for a moment and my breathing stopped dead. Finally, I heard Sky's voice but before she could deliver the rebuttal I hoped she had in mind, Flip went on.

"I have an idea, boss. Let's make a deal. Just hear me out."

The next thing I heard was Flip trying to woo her with words he had written in poetic form.

"You're the kind of girl that acts on reason; you always weigh the wrong and test the right. You take the time to tame temptation and when pleasure knocks you put up quite the fight. Sky, I know my flattery won't sway you. Of course, I know my words won't win your heart. It's awful clear that gibes and jarring won't persuade you, so let's make a deal that reason can't outsmart."

"Flip—" Sky attempted to dissuade him from making a full pitch but he silenced her by motioning with his index finger over his lips.

"Have a listen. For every date, I'll toss a lover from the bank. Give me saucy looks, I promise you'll get mine…right behind. For every smile that I get I'll give you something you can bet, and for every kiss you give, I'll give you kisses all the time. On any night you put aside for my delight, I'll invite you to my home for all the loving games you'd like. You can toy with me 'til I can't breathe a breath with any ease,' cause I'm a giver and I'd give myself to satisfy your needs."

"My friend, this is really out of order," Sky giggled.

Flip rightly took her weak opposition as an invitation to continue. "I know you think I'm a playboy of sorts and probably you question everything that I purport. But don't tell me I ain't hittin' buttons. Give me a chance and I'll give you something like romance. Give me naughty looks and I promise you'll get sweetness right behind. For every smile that I get, I'll give you things you won't forget. And for every kiss you give, I'll give you kisses all the time."

I was fitful as I pulled my ear from the door. Without realizing what I was doing, I began rapidly brushing my hands through my hair. I should have released myself from the grip of their exchange; any wise person would have never been there to begin with. A glutton for punishment, I was hooked. The torment for sneaking was about to get worse due to my pressing my ear back against the door.

"So how 'bout we start tonight?" Flip suggested.

"Look, uh, I'm flattered. But I'm over my head in work and…there may be somebody else I'm seeing."

"There's nobody else. I've checked."

"You what?"

"Unless you got something going with the skinny rich kid or his sidekick…we start with dinner, a movie; both would be great."

That was it for me, "the skinny rich kid." Sure, I was lean. Indeed, I was a rich kid. I had no shame about either but the way he spoke was intentionally degrading. I readied myself to stomp off, nearly out of my mind with rage and jealousy. My retort to the discussion would come to me later.

"I'm too busy right now, Flip. I really can't address this," Sky protested.

"You'll think about it," he smiled confidently. "Then when you're ready, we'll get our relationship moving… ever been out with a famous baseball star?"

"Flip, you need to get back to practice. I have piles of documents to review."

Sky stood up and went to open her door.

"You enjoy those flowers, dear. I'll be back for you."

I scampered off just in time. In my office, I fumed for god only knows how long. I didn't know how to handle a situation that was, in truth, none of my business. So what did I do? Something stupid, what else? I took off for her office with fire in my lungs. When I reached the closed door, I listened again, finally concluding he'd left. I knocked.

"Not you again," Sky laughed.

I opened the door. Sky stood gazing at me. Had I not been so jacked up with fury, I might have noticed the most tender, endearing and inviting gesture on her face. Instead, being filled with hatred of Flip, I proceeded like a total jerk. Sadly, that was only the beginning of my madness; I was about to let anger enjoy its normal destructive path.

"Why was Flip here?" I asked curtly.

"He wanted to talk."

"You're management and he's a player. He shouldn't be encouraged to come here just to talk."

Sky had no idea what had provoked the blunt interdiction I had ordered, nor could she have guessed why I was speaking to her with unprecedented brashness. The dearness of her smile yielded to dubitation as she tried to read me. I gave her little time, marching out as if I'd criticized her one word short of termination. I slammed the door with unintended force.

That evening at home, she tried to approach me. I told her I was wasted and needed to sleep. She examined me as if I were an alien, waiting for the Benjamin she adored to emerge from the tangle of undifferentiated affect standing in front of her.

I wanted to cry, throw myself into her arms and beg her to forgive me. Instead, I turned and went to my room to suffer regret and remorse on my own terms—what a stud.

CHAPTER 14: GROW UP; GET SOME GUTS

During the next few days, Sky and I made up. Remarkably, we accomplished cooling the air of tension without a word spoken—I guess I'd learned something about time's virtue of permitting dust to settle under rugs, sometimes forever. We discussed affairs of business. Otherwise, it was as if the incident with Flip had never happened, although I sensed that Sky was not as talented at tiptoeing around sleeping dogs as I was. She looked at me with bewilderment each time we met but refrained from embarrassing me by bringing up the topic.

Truthfully, I was not as gifted as I wished in the art of avoidance. I recognized that Flip Montel was burning a hole in my gut. After hearing him come on to Sky with more manliness than I imagined I'd ever have, I demonized him. My revilement rested only a tissue thin layer beneath my urge to strangle him—perhaps the incident about to take place was as predictable as an occasional sour note on my violin.

It happened that Sky and I were talking with one of the men working in the scouting department. He had come out of the dugout where we were standing and was showing us—mostly Sky—some paper work on a young high school kid he was convinced was going to be the next superstar of the game. Sky had already learned that the reliability of a scout was about equal to an alcoholic's promise and was listening with only one-sixteenth of one ear.

Then out of nowhere, a figure trotted over to us; it was Flip. He was beaming his normal hideous glow, so impressed with himself that he slipped his arm over Sky's shoulder. He let it linger for a few seconds and no doubt would have given it license to spend eternity there had Sky not twisted so as to release herself from his uninvited gesture.

"How's my sweet GM?" Flip rejoiced.

"We're having a meeting," I curtly informed him of what would have been obvious to anyone with even a single particle of propriety.

"No sweat," Flip answered without offense. "Just need a minute with one of my bosses—the cute one," he winked at me, a gesture that rankled me all the worse.

179

He then took Sky by the arm and directed her to stand with him, just out of earshot of our scout and me.

"Home run, double, and another two big ribbies—enough to earn me that date?"

"You earn sixty-two thousand a game; that's enough."

"Not enough for me."

"Flip, I have to go," Sky informed him, but not before surrendering to a need to laugh at his persistence.

Sky left Flip standing by himself. When she rejoined us, she immediately resumed looking over the report the scout had brought. I noticed that Flip hadn't left. Instead, he stood his ground. He wouldn't stop gaping at Sky, his mouth open so wide he looked as if he wanted to swallow her whole.

"Flip, I need a word with you," I addressed him coldly.

At that moment, Sky began walking toward the dugout with the scout following. I made my way over to where Flip was standing.

"If you have business in the future with any of us we'll be glad to take care of it, but set up a meeting with all three of us." I tried to act indifferent but inside I was having an acquaintanceship with raw emotions that I never knew existed. The skinny rich kid had built up twenty years of testosterone and was about to bat the daylights out of this baseball hotshot. "And if it's not about baseball, keep it to yourself."

It was a miracle. I imagined my body had blown up like an inflatable toy replica of Benjamin Wolf. I stood looking down on my muscled enemy, feeling if I so desired I could have taken my hands and stretched him thin as a string and then tied him in knots so complex he'd never untangle himself—I was a man! It never dawned on me to calculate that this moron might have recognized that all he needed was a pin to prick me back to size.

"Hold on," Flip chuckled, "you're jealous of my talking with Sky."

"No, Flip," I gunned at him so quickly, that I missed my own lie. "I'm telling you to leave her alone unless you have business matters to address."

"She's definitely a grown woman," Flip smirked. "I'm sure you've noticed, haven't you? Well, anyway, I'm a grown man. That said, what I do in my personal life is none of your damn business. I play for your club, buddy, but you don't own me."

"I run this team and there are rules."

"You don't run me."

"Really?" I sneered. "Why don't you take some time to think about that?"

"I don't need time."

"Then think about this. You're suspended. And Flip, don't come back until you agree to my terms."

It was unbelievable. I was pumped, so high I might have taken his place in the lineup and cracked a couple big ones myself. I didn't feel afraid. I didn't feel anger. I didn't feel disgust. I didn't feel ashamed or remorseful. I didn't feel anything—that was the problem. I was flying without controls and soon had to force land under inauspicious conditions.

"You can't do that," Flip bellowed arrogantly. "I've got a contract, you idiot."

"Your contract doesn't say you have to play."

"My agent will have your bony ass," he jeered, pausing to deliberate whether or not to divulge a suspicion. "You really think I ever bought that nonsense about Gypsy Dust? I *know* why this team is winning."

There was a hint of threat in his voice as he raced off through the dugout. I wandered about the field wondering what if anything he had figured out about the team's success. *He couldn't know about the music?* I assured myself.

Then my mind made a sharp right turn. *What did I go and do that for?* I muttered to the only soul present, me. *He's right, it's none of my business if he wants to date Sky and she's interested in him. One of these days… sometime I've got to stop this lie. I'm going to have to face reality.* I stopped and instinctively posed a question. *Is this something resembling love? Is this the state of mind and passion that causes man to lose his sense of reason?*

It was that single statement, *this has to be somethin' like love* that repeated in my head a thousand times. Then I noticed my internal dialogue turning into phrases that might have mimicked Flip in that I was composing my own lyrics.

"I get excited when she kids me, I'll confess. And I fall into silence when she taunts me with finesse. Who would call it friendship when the signs all go against it? If it aches the very core of me, it's something like love.

"I always smile when she stares into my eyes and I can't control the high I get when she flatters me with lies. How can I be so blind to this and drive off all the signs? If it moves the very heart of me, it's somethin' like love.

"I gotta do somethin', I'm stuck inside somethin' like love. So quick and sudden, I'm stuck inside somethin' like love. It hurts to say but I'm in shame in somethin' like love.

"I start to whimper when she's hounded on by men, the confident aggressive types who flaunt their ill-intent. How long can I deny that I'm in fear more than resent, and that I lack the courage to do somethin?"

My mind hit a writer's block. I stood in desperation pondering my deplorable state. Then my inert brain began cranking, spitting out words I was barely ready to hear.

"I think Sky's had the answer all along. I just need to grow up, get some guts."

Truth must be contagious…I was about to make a full confession.

"I've always had to take the friendliest of paths with her but how can I get past the fact that I want more than laughs with her. I want to wake up in the morning and be wrapped with her, passionately grasping her so I can happily bask in her. Why can't I have it, the whole entire thing? From time to time, she flirts with me and that's a start I think. It's time for me to face the day that I've been fearing of. I've gotta do somethin' or I'm stuck with somethin' like love."

I just need to grow up, get some guts. No kidding, I sighed.

I was aimlessly strolling on the field, when Sky came out of the dugout and ran over to me.

"What happened? Flips in there packing his locker," she reported excitedly. "Ben, he said you suspended him."

"That's right, I did."

"Why?"

"Nothing. Just for nothing."

"Nothing! What is going on with you, Ben? You're not yourself anymore. Besides, we're running this team together. Don't you think I have a right to know everything about our players?"

"You do," I answered robotically. "I'm screwing up right now. I'm sorry."

"At least tell me what's wrong," she pled. "Ben, I care for you."

"It's just some things I have to work out," is all I managed to mutter.

"Like what? We're on top of the world. Let's not allow success to ruin us."

"I'll explain later." Then I stopped before dropping

what I suspected might be a nuclear device. "We may have a more immediate problem. I'm fairly certain that Flip knows about the music—at least he's suspicious that we're doing something that's inspiring the players beyond their normal ability."

"Why? He could never figure it out."

"Just tell Whitman to meet us at Ripley's later this afternoon. We can discuss it then."

"Ben, I don't like what you're doing. You're scaring me. I've never seen you so distant, so unreachable."

Guts? In an instant, they'd abandoned me like a friend when you go bankrupt.

"I have a couple things I need to look into," I said pleasantly...and gutlessly. "I'll be at the bar later."

By the time I arrived, Sky and Whitman had taken a table. Whitman, however, was sharing a dance with Kona. When I came in, they paused. Then, they walked close to the table.

"Benny, Sky, come join us," Whitman called out.

"In a bit, Whit," I answered.

"I took Kona to the game last night," Whitman informed us.

"Great," I smiled.

"I told Whit I'd date him after the season, if The Blue Stripes won. But they're doing so well...it's not a big cheat that we started early, would you say?" Kona giggled.

"Not even a chisel," I joked. "Glad you're both having a good time."

"It's been fun...but Kona tells me that if The Blue Stripes lose, she's taking back everything she's given me," Whitman said zanily.

"I'd like to be there to watch that," Sky responded, even more farcically.

"Well, too bad it'll never happen. Nothing can stop this team," he guaranteed as he looked into Kona's eyes.

"Kona, I hate to interfere but would you mind if we have a few words alone with Whitman?" Sky asked.

"We just lost Flip," Sky rifled at Whit the second Kona left.

"How?"

"I suspended him."

"Why?"

"Well...we had a disagreement."

"Mild-mannered, Ben," Whitman teased as he poked his massive fist into my shoulder. "You got pushed over the edge by that cavalier prick. What did he do, try to screw Sky?"

"Whitman, he'd have less of a chance than you," Sky bantered back.

"She's still yours, Ben."

Whitman had the ability to see with his heart. The insinuations he'd lob at me were his signals that he recognized the lust I had for her, an infatuation Sky either was blind to or, as I suspected, didn't want to address due to not wanting to crush me.

"Anyway, no objection from me, Ben. Getting rid of Flip may be for the better."

"Right. Thorne will take him in a second," I answered.

"I know he will too," Sky agreed. "But this is big. We'll need to get some help."

"No problem," Whitman offered. "I'll call Karlov."

"Exactly, what I was thinking," Sky agreed.

"I hope we can catch him between drinks," I jested.

"There is no between for my professor."

"He'll be here in a while," Whitman informed us after a brief talk with Karlov. Then he waved to Kona, motioning for her to come back.

"One more round with my honey," Whitman winked.

Sky and I sat silently at the table. I could hardly lift my eyes for fear they'd travel to the same outpost in space as hers. The spell was broken as Whitman moments later rushed over to us.

"The real estate we need to dump just walked in. You won't believe it," Whitman informed us breathlessly. "He's with Thorne."

Whitman then nodded in the direction of Thorne and Flip, now standing at the bar. Sky grabbed both of us by the arm and directed us to a table far off to the corner of the establishment where we couldn't be seen by either man.

"They'll never know we're here," she howled like a college kid after a prank.

The ensuing minutes unfolded as if this were a scene from a musical comedy. If at the moment I could have been a small bird sitting on Thorne's shoulder, I would have been in for an earful.

"Don't worry, Flip. They have to trade you," Thorne assured him.

"They'd never let me go to your team; you know that, Reed."

"I have deals with them that will preclude them trading you to anyone else. Trust me on this one, young fellow," Thorne bragged. "You think old man Wolf is going to let you sit on the bench for ten mil a year?"

"Makes no sense, but look what he did to the team. That made no sense either."

"Flip, those kids have been lucky so far, that's all there is to it. And with you off their roster, they'll need more than good fortune." Thorne puckered his lips. "I have a lot riding on this and I'm about to make a killing."

"What do you mean?"

"It's not important." Thorne's replied briskly. "Just keep playing for me the way you are now and there won't be a problem."

"Well," Flip said hesitantly, "that's what I have to go over with you. You see, the way I'm playing is better than I am."

"You're twenty-eight. You're in your prime. I'd expect

this to be your best season. It should be no surprise to you either."

"But it's not me," Flip said lamentably.

"Of course," Thorne patronized him. "Somebody else has crawled inside your body…who do you think it might be, Jolting Joe DiMaggio back from the dead, or a revived Alex Rodriguez?"

"No. It's not like that," Flip insisted. "It's this music—"

"Music? What music are we talking about?"

"They have this music; it plays all the time. If we're in the clubhouse, in the exercise room, working out on the field, in the dugout, during the game…you name it; even when we travel they control the music. This is not music you'd hear on the radio or purchase online…you can't buy it," Flip reported. "Nobody pays any attention. They all think it's just different songs created by Wolf's kid. But I know there's something about it that is different, like a drug that heightens your performance. You want to know why I'm better than ever, why this team of nobodies is winning? That's the answer."

"Flip, I thought you were one of the few level-headed, commonsense men in baseball who didn't go for this sort of magical thinking."

"Believe me, I am. This is not a supernatural power at play, and I promise no bearded wizards are dancing in the clubhouse. This is science. Those kids are smart," Flip punctuated the last word. "They may think a home run means you're having a pizza delivered to your house but other than baseball they're whizzes."

"You're serious?" Thorne cackled.

"You know how bad The Stripes are. But we're beating the socks off you guys, and everybody else. They have this team so dazzled, they're believing in themselves."

"Okay," Thorne consented, "I'll look into it."

"I've got to have that music. I know that's what it is; there's nothing else it could be."

"Flip, if you have to have it, if it's that powerful…well, then I just may have some for myself."

"Can you get it?" Flip posed imploringly.

"Can I get it?" Thorne mimicked. "I'll do whatever it takes…so, Mr. Wolf thinks he can have his way with me."

Thorne took his drink down in one gulp, deposing the glass on the bar top.

"Let me tell you a little story," Thorne gloated. "Yes, I'm going to get him. That's what I have in mind. A man like Wolf can be your friend one moment and your enemy the next. Just hear me out here, Flip."

"What happened?" Flip asked eagerly.

"Once upon an autumn day, I had a friend I'd never trade, a real class act, the kind who'd never leave your periled back. For months and years I showed my passion…nights would find us late in action. Laughing, yes. But we were working hard with the burden of stress." Thorne grimaced. "Then just past Halloween, he dropped me for some hallow scheme. He left me on the streets to see his child take my throne in heed.

"Well, I may be a hard-ass man but he's the hardest son of a bitch a man could ever know. So just consider it solved. I'll stop at nothing to watch him crawl." Thorne's face took on a demonic glare. "With a little bit of patience, we'll take him. All of my rage will assuage when I break him. And with a little bit of wit, we'll efface him; lay him on the road to a bottomless basin. Flipper, with a little fighting, we'll strike him. All of my wants will be stomped when he's griping. Oh, to see him on his knees begging me to give into mercy and grant him reprieve.

"Hah! Wolf is an evil bum who thinks himself a noble one. So marvelous, sent to spot the slightest slip and harp on it." Thorne paused before making a proud admission of dishonorableness. "Well, sure I've broken some rules, told some lies and sold some jewels. I've even gone behind his back at times to make a deal or two. But I've never claimed to be a straight-edged man whose record is clean. Okay, I'll admit it. I've always been the type to cheat when there's a time or need…anyway, I'm way off course. The point of all this long discourse is simply that you need not fright, the music's in my narrow sight."

"You really think you can get it?" Flip queried in disbelief.

Thorne took out his cell phone and punched in numbers.

"Ben, it's been a while," Thorne addressed me when

I answered—he had no idea I was only a few feet away from him.

"Mr. Thorne, I didn't think I'd hear from you this soon."

"You're in a jam, sonny. I can help you out if you let me."

"That's thoughtful of you, sir," I said politely.

"We can settle this right now if you care to. I'm at Ripley's. Why don't you bring that girlfriend and the brute with you and meet in…say an hour?"

The comical nature of what was happening helped me completely forget the tension that was still thick between Sky and me. I mimed to Sky and Whitman that it was Thorne and that he wanted to meet…at Ripley's. They were gagging with laughter, so much so the infectiousness of their spirit left me hardly able to respond to Thorne.

"I think we can do that," I eked out before hanging up.

"Ripley's in an hour," I repeated out loud to Sky and Whitman.

"Let me call Karlov back and tell him to get over here now," Whitman suggested.

We passed the hour having a beer and talking like old times, neither Sky nor I wishing to ruin the good feeling of the moment by bringing up unfinished business. Just before the dial on the wall clock made the full revolution, Flip left. He never noticed us sitting jubilantly at the table in the corner. Within a few minutes, Karlov arrived. Whitman had assumed the responsibility to be the lookout. He spotted his teacher as soon as he came in the door. He ran over to him and directed Karlov to our table.

"What is going on? I've given all of you pointers here and there but you're in first place and that's a mistake. By my calculations, at best your team should be ingloriously competing for the cellar."

"Sir, there are some classified matters we couldn't let you in on," Whitman informed him.

"Classified matters? Listen to you, sounding like a big shot," Karlov coughed. "Get me a drink before I pass out; the throat is parched."

"Can you wait a few minutes?" Sky appealed. "We need you one hundred percent present for this."

"Okay, but I think if I'm to have a role here I should know everything."

"Sorry, sir. We can't do it. If you would, please, just trust me that it's our stupid little secret and it won't affect the negotiation we need to complete."

"All right, Whitman. Let's get with it...I'm terribly thirsty."

"I just want to go over one thing first," Sky mentioned. "Professor Karlov, you've provided valuable input statistically but this is a business matter. I know you've spent your life in academia...can you—?"

"This game boils down to nothing but numbers; it's all in the numbers!" Karlov stated emphatically.

Suddenly, from his usual languorous self, he seemed animated. Perfunctorily he pulled off his coat and tossed it to Sky, and then to our mutual amazement he buzzed around us while we sat, slinging an impromptu discourse on…numbers.

"It's all in the numbers, kids. This business always comes down to the same thing…numbers. See, if a guy's a star at third but then in left field he's flat because he always sighs at fly balls, there's a number for that. And if he hits the ball a mile but he never hits the gap, in recent years they've found a brand new number for that. If he possesses piles of talent but in clutch times he's inept, you can bet your bottom dollar there's a number for that. And if the fellow is always silent in the season's latter half, you can fiddle with the figures and find a number for that too.

"Ah, the game's a festival of scientific facts and every circumstance you study has numbers amassed." Karlov smiled confidently. "It's just a matter now of tying things intact and this negotiation will be simple as a snap… you see, when I need one for any reason to beat this sap, there'll be a number for that.

"You kids starting to understand how this is a game us academicians can play? How about a few more examples? When sluggers summon hits but swing at every dreadful pitch it sends a sign through a little number you'll find. Then when the season is done and the final battles come, those who starred may be marred and there's a number for that. Remember this, any time illusion plays a role and leaves you ruined, you should know that numbers would have thrown the lies asunder.

"As I said, the game is a festival of science. So know that when I go on to meet this low pawn, I wanna see him trapped and numbers will do that. Yes, I can take him down with intellect 'til he's a quiver from a wreck and all I need to make him crack is simple stats."

We were awed. Hiding in Karlov's soul was an enthusiastic entertainer? The thought gave me faith that a miracle might befall me some day and I could become a gutsy guy like Flip. None of us had seen Karlov as spirited and energized as he was during the brief lecture.

"Professor, you pull this off and you're definitely on the team," Sky promised. "But you're going to have to let me style you up a bit."

"I'm not stylish enough?" he absurdly retorted in an outfit fit for a vagrant.

"You're not at all stylish," Sky blurted out. "But once you are, the ladies are going to have to watch out."

"Including you?" Karlov questioned.

Jesus Christ. Was I being punished? Now Karlov had the hots for her.

Sky then briefed Karlov on our situation regarding Flip. When she finished Whitman tapped him on the arm, pointing across the room.

"The bar wraps around that corner and Thorne is over there."

Karlov rose and with uncharacteristic precision of gait followed in my footsteps as I lead our incongruous assembly to where Thorne was standing with a beer in his hand.

"Shall we take a table?" I suggested.

"I'm fine as is," Thorne answered. "Do my best thinking on my feet." He glanced inquiringly at Karlov. "Who's that?"

"He's one of Whitman's professors. Occasionally he helps us with team matters. He is our consultant," I informed him.

"You teach finance over at The Institute?" Thorne assumed, reaching to shake with Karlov.

"No, I'm a neurokinetic scientist."

"I can see how you could be a great asset. Perhaps they'll make you a GM also," Thorne chided. He gazed about the room as if in a state of disgusted disbelief. "Well, let's get right to it. You need to unload Flip Montil…and let's face it, with the pending deal we have, nobody else will be able to take him off your hands. Now, I'm willing to compensate—"

"Pending…deal?" Karlov stammered. "Oh, that," he vaguely added.

"I'm sure your partners detailed this for you."

"Indeed, they did."

"So you know that Flip is mine regardless—"

"Not unless you beat us and right now we hold a solid edge," Whit reminded him.

"You've had some early season breaks," Thorne snickered. "Down the stretch, the story changes. Does it really matter, though? Flip is worthless to you now and for the duration of his contract."

"True. But then let's cut to the chase. Mr. Thorne, you want this as bad as The Blue Stripes."

"Look, you may be a professor of neuro…whatever it is, but this is baseball. They have a player making ten big ones a year, every year for another six. Worse, he won't lift a bat ever again for his team. You want a lawsuit over this? Now tell me who needs this deal more."

"Let's say—"

"Doc, let's say I do them a huge favor and take Flip off your hands now rather than at the end of the year. And for a rental fee, I'm prepared to throw in a pair of prime triple-AAA steer."

"Thinking too narrow," Karlov counseled. "You have a malignancy in right field. Hanratty is wobbling on one leg; it won't hold until the end of the year. Then, you're about to lose part of you bullpen, right?"

"How do you—?'

"I follow the game, Mr. Thorne. I make it my business to know about every team. Now, we are prepared to let you take Flip, but we want to toss in Hill and Mason as well. They'll fill in your holes; look at the year they're having in spite of their threat to retire. In return, all I want is Chipper…and about two million cash because we're giving you a chance to make a comeback." Karlov paused to let the proposed terms settle in on Thorne. "I know it's generous but…we all want this matter to get settled as soon as possible."

In spite of Karlov's explanation, Thorne was no fool. Immediately a grin of resistance could be observed. But before he even had an opportunity to rebut Karlov, Sky invited herself into the negotiations.

"Wait a second," she hotly interjected, appearing peeved. "I'm sorry Mr. Thorne but I need to talk with the professor…alone."

She took Karlov aside. As I watched the exchange, I would have guessed by her body language that she was giving our advisor a serious tongue whipping. She appeared furious with him.

"What are you doing?" Sky forcefully asserted to Karlov. She was acting a part, convincingly expressing her appall for Thorne's entertainment while delighted with the position Karlov was bargaining. "It's a great deal," she shot out so that only Karlov could hear. I agree it's perfect."

"I'm a little confused here. Then what are you so worked up over," Karlov asked.

"I could see that he was about to reject the offer."

"At first he will, of course," Karlov explained.

"It was more than at first. But if he believes I'm against it, he'll start thinking it's more attractive. By the time we get back there, I want to see a lot less of that skeptical look on his arrogant face."

"Sweet."

"This is as sweet a deal as we can get, Karlov. Hill and Mason will not perform as well for them as for us; trust me on this one," Sky chuckled.

"Chipper is a different sort of player. He's versatile and predictable as baby drool. You'll be able to trade him for a lot more than you're paying."

"I'm definitely taking you shopping," Sky smiled. "Come on. Let's finish off Thorne before he chokes on his bile."

As they were on their way returning to join us, Sky's roll-playing dubitation over the position Karlov had taken continued.

"Maybe I need to go over this in more detail with Whitman and Ben," she cautioned loud enough for us to hear.

"Trust me," Karlov argued back. Then without further consideration of Sky's concerns, he addressed Thorne. "Just a little jitters on my friend's part. Still, I think we can get this matter wrapped up."

"Sure," Thorne agreed, nodding his head but with less uncertainty than he displayed earlier. "I don't want to be here all day." Then Thorne reached out to shake hands, first with Karlov, followed by Sky, Whitman, and finally me. "I'm good with this deal if you all agree."

"Believe me, Mr. Thorne. It's the best medicine for both of us."

"I tend to agree, professor. And good luck to all of you for the rest of the season."

Thorne took off, his haughty demeanor returning as he no doubt couldn't wait to express his glee that once again he had duped us—Sky and Karlov had a different take.

"We did it! We did it! We did it!" Karlov celebrated.

"I'm assuming you got the better of the bargain," I addressed Sky. She grinned broadly. "Wait until my dad hears this one. You are amazing."

"And you're on your way to amazing," she needlessly complimented.

"Certainly you deserve credit for being amazing as well, professor," I gifted Karlov.

Watching the stream of approbations, Whitman had his own take. "Wow, baseball does amazing things to people."

CHAPTER 15: THE BURGLARY

We had come a long way from nowhere and undoubtedly helped the team get to their current level of play.

Whitman had discovered a new scientific app for the great research patented by Mr. Lowery in the acoustics field. I contributed by composing a collection of new sounds and beats designed to conceal the hidden commands instructing our players to be better than they could have otherwise been. Sky had developed the mathematical models to test and interpret the outcome of our experiments.

We had successfully peddled Flip and his large salary, and then, in our opinion, turned around the potential beating we anticipated at the hands of Thorne—the bet was still on irrespective of where Flip was playing. Better still, we now had access to Karlov, a dream of an asset in terms of dealing with the subtleties of player management and trades. Sure, I had put us in a spot with Flip but Karlov and Sky had successfully capitalized on the situation to improve our overall lineup.

What did we have to worry about? That was the problem. When you have nothing that concerns you, that's generally when you're most vulnerable...and we had pathetically let our guard down. For three kids supposed to be so bright, we had exposed our inexperience in a frightfully dangerous way.

How? We had a secret weapon that was legal, ethical and moral, a power source that any other team would have paid millions to get their hands on. What did we do to protect it? Nothing. Whitman, a tech master who wouldn't write a paper in school without having it backed up on his email and then in the cloud, treated our entire program with the carelessness of a worn out pair of tennis shoes.

Every night he'd pack up shop, leaving everything pertaining to our system locked in his office. Indeed, he backed it up but what he never did, and what none of us suggested, was to be sure that the data generated from our research, and the models we were using, could never land in the hands of friends or enemies.

After Flip disclosed to Thorne his premise that the music was the key to a group of lame players performing like All-Stars, Thorne went to work on a plan of attack. He was a man who didn't need to deliberate the line demarcating right from wrong. Hell, his lack of scruples permitted him to kick the border separating legal from illegal in either direction—his determination to win had no bounds, especially in this case where he was thirsting to sock my father in the belly.

Our offices were located in a building owned by Sir Wolf. We had a security officer on duty round the clock but the man was as worried about an intruder as the hiccups. Most of the evening when he wasn't sleeping he was studying for classes he took during the daytime. Occasionally, he'd perfunctorily wander the halls and check that interior and exterior doors were locked.

One evening a tall, thin, hooded figure dressed in a black tight-fit top and pant outfit used a device to open the secondary door on the fourteenth floor of our building. The Blue Stripes occupied three full floors. The one he chose, not by chance, was the one housing Whitman's office.

No doubt Thorne had done his research, likely bribing one of our employees for information, though we never determined if that was the case. What we did find out, but sadly some time later, was that we had been burglarized.

The man crept through the hallway and then with ease unlatched the lock on Whitman's door. Once inside, he began his handiwork. He sat in front of Whitman's computer, turning it on and then performing a few functions. He then took a small box-shaped object out of the case he was carrying and with a cable he had brought with him he connected it to the computer. Again he tapped instructions on the keyboard and performed a few functions before he hit, "Return."

As the machine was in the process of a full backup of Whitman's entire collection of files pertaining to our Magic Music project, the man waited. He picked up a bat resting in the corner of the room and began taking practice swings. It might have appeared to be a Chaplinesque comedy routine as he swung awkwardly at an imaginary ball, his body nearly falling over with each thrust of the bat. He may have been a great sleuth but was as bad as any of us with a bat.

The man became so engrossed in his play that he was startled when he heard a low buzzing sound, reminding him that the task he had been hired to carry out was completed. He placed the bat back where he found it and then examined the screen. He instructed the machine once again and waited a short time. Under his head cover he smiled, satisfied that all had gone so smoothly.

He disconnected the cord through which he had sucked the lifeblood out of Whitman's computer and placed it, along with the small box back, in the satchel he'd brought with him. Finally, he locked the door from inside and left. As he started to make his way down the hall he noticed a dim light burning at the end, next to the stairwell he planned to descend by foot. He moved silently in that direction but was relieved to find it was only our security man, in deep meditation.

We had no way of knowing that we now had a partner, the archenemy, Thorne. The situation now favored Thorne. We were in the worst position possible, ignorant of the danger we were facing and with an adversary able to clobber us at will. After all, Thorne had by far the better team and he was about to make music that would increase their effectiveness. He had to be busting his gut anticipating the beating he planned for us.

We were busting our guts too, on top of the world, living in the pages of a fairy tale Thorne was about to set ablaze.

CHAPTER 16: ELVES CAN BE SINISTER

A few weeks had passed since the covert operation conducted for Thorne. During that period of time, he'd been employing a team of tech geniuses of his own to discern every detail of the advantage he now owned equally with us. We had been watching our position in the standings very gradually begin to slip. It might have been cause for concern, but the data looked good so Sky concluded it was a slight downturn that had to be predictable in that nothing in life stays consistent—she was a math and stat giant and lived by laws of probability such that no condition or circumstance shocked her.

One evening we all decided to take in a game together. We had access to my father's box at the top of the stadium but we all preferred sitting at the field level on the third base line. I had just returned with drinks for all of us. Up to this point, I still hadn't made progress addressing my relationship with Sky. I'd say she had given up on the prospect of a more candid discussion with me except that I sensed a subtle undercurrent of irritation coming from her toward me that had never been there before.

When I handed her a cup, she took a sip. "Ben, you got me diet. You know I'm drinking regular," she nipped at me.

"Wait," I cried out. "The last time you got upset because I was supposed to get you diet."

"You're swinging late on the ball."

Her comment was chilly, lacking any of the playfulness I was used to with her. When I put Whitman's drink by his side, he was chatting with a couple sitting next to him and seemed not to be listening to Sky and me. The hurt it caused me knowing she was irked with me, must have set off an alarm because I was about to have a heart-to-heart with her.

"Look, Sky, I've been meaning to talk to you."

"I'm sorry, Ben. Maybe I'm a little tense about the team. I don't mean to take it out on you."

"I know. Still, I need to tell you something."

"About what?"

I had no idea where the courage was coming from but I wanted to come clean about Flip, at least to let her know that I had argued with him and that I didn't approve of him having personal relationships with any of us.

"Remember the day I suspended Flip and—"

Whitman must have been listening with one ear tuned to our conversation.

"You sound like my parents. 'Herman,'" he mimicked, 'you know I don't like to have sex before dinner.'"

It was Whitman who always knew where my passion dwelled; he never missed an opportunity to dare me to venture further than the tin heart I owned permitted. As he finished his comment to us, he noticed an attractive blond standing off to the side; he motioned for her to come to where he sat.

"We'll talk later, Sky," I mentioned.

Suddenly the urge to try and get more intimate with her abandoned me. Sky didn't respond but she sported a mystified pose on her face.

"I guess I shouldn't be surprised running into you here," the attractive girl said to Whitman.

"Guys, this is our neighbor, Merci."

We greeted her but she seemed far more interested in Whitman.

"If you're free after the game would you like to come over?" she invited with irresistible provocation.

"It's a date," Whitman declared.

Merci left. Whitman was in his glory.

"Over a year we've lived in our building and she's

never looked at me. You've seen her, right?" he asked to both of us.

"I thought I recognized her," I said.

"Well, now she's mine, just like that," he said with a snap of his fingers.

"That should teach you something," Sky suggested.

"I'm a lot better looking than I thought," Whitman swaggered.

"We all know that. But with this one, if she falls in love with you it will be for luxury and not looks," Sky notified him.

"What's the difference? I've got them both," Whitman gloated.

"Well, to get you off your mountain, Mr. Lady's Man, did you talk with Karlov?"

"Yes. He said the results don't add up. In his words, 'Thorne's team can't be playing as well as they are.'"

"You think Hill and Mason are better than we thought?" I asked.

"Not at all." Whitman had his computer with him and opened it. "Here's Karlov's data. After Mason, Hill and Flip went to Thorne, their performance slumped exactly as we would have predicted. Then a few weeks later, they made a total rebound. That was exactly when their entire team started to outperform their prior numbers."

"No explanation?" Sky wondered.

"He said he'd keep looking into it. Then he said he smelled something foul."

"Did he indicate what he meant by that?" she persisted.

"There's no number for what's happening," Whitman quoted Karlov. I noticed Whitman punching his computer a bit more forcefully than usual before continuing. "When there's no number, Karlov can't accept it." Whitman now started banging on the keyboard. "Damn it! This keeps happening."

"What's going on?" Sky posed.

"It's been acting up for weeks but keeps getting worse. It repeats forcing itself into an automatic download function and won't stop," Whitman explained. "I'll take it to the geeks at school and let them have a look."

It was the seventh inning stretch. The music I'd written was playing. The crowd was energetic.

"Is our music special? Look what it does to people." Sky bragged. "Fellows, we still need to figure out what we're going to do to slow down Thorne's charge. Any ideas?"

"I don't have any but what if I run it past my father? He's been in the baseball business for years. Besides, it's about time we share a little of what we're doing with him."

"It's fine with me, Ben."

"Me too," said Whitman who had packed up the computer, along with its misbehavior, and was getting ready to leave. "What's to worry about when the sky is vanilla and miles of Merci's are lined up for dates with His Majesty?"

"Absolutely nothing," Sky placated him.

The following day, my father was in his office. I wasn't sure how much I wanted to disclose to him or for that matter what I expected he might add that could help explain the peculiar figures and unexpected performance of Thorne's team.

When I arrived, the secretary notified me that he had company, but she announced me just the same. He instructed her to let me in. When I opened the door, he was with Mayor Tollini.

"Fred, you know my son, Ben?"

"I've been watching The Stripes. It's one hell of a job you're doing, Ben."

"Thank you, sir. I must explain that this success would have never happened without both of my partners, Sky and Whitman."

"My son, as you can tell, is modest."

"No shame admitting to needing help," Tollini commented. "Look, Arnold, I need to be rushing off to another meeting but we'll stay in touch about this matter. Good to see you, Ben."

"Come take a look," my dad insisted as soon as The Mayor left.

He led me to another room where he had piled stacks of drawings, the one on top a picture of a new stadium.

"It's the plan for the new ballpark." My dad could

barely contain his pride. "I finally have those bastards by the balls. It's all about patience, son. I let the fans argue my case while I threatened enough legal action against the league they were peeing in their pants. Now, all of a sudden, the city is pushing through a special tax relief bill to fund the park—it's going to mean at least a huge increase in the worth of the property."

"So, we're making money regardless of how we perform?" I queried.

"Hell no. You're still losing money but it doesn't hurt when the asset value is jumping sky high," he bubbled. "There's always more than one way to skin the old cat."

"Oh. Well, I'm not sure I get it but I wanted to discuss a little problem with you."

"Then perk up my furry friend. Little problems I handle on the spot. It's the big ones that require loans. Come. Sit down and talk to me."

"You know how well we're doing—"

"You worried that bastard Thorne could be a spoiler?"

"That's what I wanted to talk about with you."

"I told you it's a harsh world out there, Ben. You can't blame a rat for eating cheese."

"Let me tell you a couple of things first."

"I'm listening, my boy…and by god, you haven't talked much to me about the job."

"Dad, I'm leaving the team after this season. I tried—"

"You did," he declared imperially.

As his words were delivered, and I was awaiting him

magnanimously letting me know I had all the time I needed to find the killer instinct in myself, Whitman rapped on the door. He stood at the threshold, appearing agitated.

"Sit down. Sit down, Whitman," my dad instructed when he saw him. "No secrets with best friends. Anyway, Ben, I saw it coming. You never loved this business and never will." Then he turned to Whitman, his words astonishing me. "And the same goes for you, young man. Baseball, running the affairs of a business, is not your calling in life. A man has to make peace with himself."

"You're right, sir."

"Let me tell both of you something at the same time. Took me a lot of suffering to figure this one out. I'll offer it to both of you free of charge. One of the most important assignments in life is getting what you truly need. One of the most difficult accomplishments in life is figuring out what those indispensables are. Sometimes you have to journey to far-off lands to learn that your home is in your backyard. You're both going to do wonderful things in life."

My father had bestowed on me a greater gift than the entire empire he ruled over. I felt like crying. I might have too had Whitman not forged ahead with his agenda.

"Mr. Wolf, the reason we're winning is that we invented a new sort of music; we call it Magic Music but in truth it's purely scientific."

"Dad," I interrupted Whitman, "it makes our players perform better."

"You're serious?" he asked, to which we both nodded we were. "Well, I'll be damned!" he rejoiced. "If you're sure it works, it might be worth more than a baseball franchise."

"I don't know about that but we want to win this year...I mean go all the way. You see, sir, Sky—"

"Whitman, I know about the little lady. No need to say a word."

"But the problem is that all of a sudden Thorne's team is playing catch up and we haven't been able to figure out how," Whitman explained. "Now I might have a clue—"

Sky had been looking for us and was notified where we were. She walked in, cutting Whitman off mid-sentence.

"We killed them on those trades," she protested. "None of those players could be doing as well as they are, especially all of them together. They have the music. I'm sure of it."

"Funny you bring this up. I may have some information that you'll find interesting," my father offered. "I have friends—some in the right places. Well, a few are positioned so that they can peek in on what dear Thorne is up to."

"Like a plant," Sky surmised.

"Stealth is fair; theft and murder are not," my dad lectured. "Some rules are there for the benefit of the whole and you don't want to break those. But on the subject of

Thorne, it just so happens that I was recently informed of a strange change at his facility. All of the players on his team were given new musical tapes and instructed to listen to them...hell, I never gave it much thought before you brought this up. But what if—"

"How? It's not possible they wandered by chance onto what we created," Sky objected.

"That's what I'm trying to get to," Whitman said with renewed excitation. "Remember when my computer was on the fritz? I took it over to the lab and after they finished with it they concluded that somebody broke into the system and copied the entire hard drive. That's why it's malfunctioning. They made a mistake and left a command...like a virus...that keeps growing; the larger it gets, the more it orders the repetition of the identical function."

"I told you Flip had indicated that he had figured out why our team was performing so well. He had to tell Thorne and from there it's obvious what happened."

"Ben, he's that big a schmuck to break in and steal our music files," Sky asserted.

"Karlov told me we were missing an essential fact and once we found it everything would come together," Whitman added. "It's my fault. I was so hyped on what we were doing, I never took the proper precautions to protect us."

While Whitman was commencing to flog himself,

my father's imposing figure was motoring around the office.

"I told you, Ben, he's an evil one. Ah, but am I a man to stand by and watch him swindle you precious three?" It was a rhetorical question and he proceeded accordingly. "Take off the gloves, boys…and girls too. Listen up while I explain how screwed Thorne just became." My dad appeared in a trance-like state, swooning to what must have been an inner beat. "Yeah, that's what I'm looking for…that little feeling. You see kids, Wolf's sensitive side is a bit more complex than it seems on the surface."

"I can't wait to see," Sky egged him on.

"Well, I often feel a pain inside for elder men with sickly lives—a warm affection for what beckons as their days pass by. In fact, it's not uncommon that I comment when I see an injury even if the player hurt is playing for a rival team. And I'll disclose that my heart goes out to those who pout for loss of love and family; to those souls who weep and grieve, I humbly say I'm sorry."

His congeniality swiftly transformed to harshness.

"But not a person on this earth could ever make me feel the hurt that I command for any man who steals a dime from me." He paused to punctuate a cautionary note that at first seemed directed to nobody in particular, but soon took aim on the intended object. "Felons heed my warning for you will surely hear me roaring down your back with a dagger and a laugh."

Like a stage actor, he returned to a more amiable tone. "You see kids, I'm quite old-fashioned, a proponent of a true rationalist. So I believe an eye for an eye is always fair. But sometimes I go too far; lose an eye and it makes me tart, so rather than a fair reply I take the whole damn face in stride. But can you blame me? I'm not the worst of kinds. There's surely other men instead who'd take the thief's entire head." He stopped to stare at each of us separately before completing his speech. "That's why I feel sorry that man who crossed my darling three young chums—he's the one I truly pity on this day."

The three of us sat silently. I'd heard the swish-swash-bang-boom-I-am-your-nightmare, I-am-your-doom roar of this giant many times in the past…they hadn't.

"Mr. Wolf," Whitman eventually squeaked, "what are you going to do?"

"See this?" my dad asked as he picked up his check-book. "The Wolf bank is open for business."

"We're still very tight on money. I didn't even have my hair done this week," Sky informed him with a smirk. "But really, Mr. Wolf, we're not in a position to borrow and we know the rules."

"Rules? New lesson, cream puff…oh, forget what I said…you've got a team in contention and because of what you've done this year, I've got this city and the league in a bear hug. Fortunes are being made as we speak," he pronounced solemnly. Next he dropped the checkbook on to the table, commencing to tear out one after another the individual checks, shredding them, and letting the pieces scatter on the floor. "Checks. Checks. Checks! As many as you need."

"We do have the two million from the trade for Flip," Sky recollected."

"You'll need a lot more than that if you have to go at Thorne on an even playing field." My dad laughed deviously. "The trade deadline is Wednesday, is it not?"

"It is," Sky answered.

"Big meeting coming up with all your colleagues. Find a way to spend yourself to a winner. Get out there, kids. Buy. Buy. Buy!"

"We'll have to see—"

"See what, Sky? Don't see a thing. You have *fuck- you* money. You know what that is?" We all sat mute, though I chuckled since I had heard him define it many times. "That's the money that allows you to say *fuck you* to anyone who tries to get in the way of your good deeds. Now go rock him, sock him…destroy that rascal!!"

None of us were talking. My father's mind was in fifth gear. "Now you'll need a top third baseman to replace Flip, one more starting pitcher and…I promise you, Whitman, once I have you talking to my people on the technological details of these sounds, we'll plug his music with a new tune that will deafen his boys. It's war."

Whitman raised his right arm, pointing ecstatically with his index finger to signal to my father that he'd be right back. He ran out of the room and a couple minutes later returned. He had on a pushcart several huge bound volumes of what looked like old-fashioned computer printouts. He hoisted one of the books and held it aloft as he spoke.

"Sir, I have a good idea what we need to do. Karlov and I have been studying statistical data on every infielder in the majors and triple-AAA." The elevation in his level of thrill was evident in the raised volume of his voice and the accelerated delivery of his speech. "Using combinational topography and applying to it infinitesimal geometry, I've developed a formula to determine the best defensive players." He threw down the folder and replaced it with another similar version.

"What makes hitters better? I'm developing a method using common acoustical-optical physics along with elliptical functions to address it; it's near completed. Every time the pitcher throws the ball it has its own timbre, frequency and pitch, a unique sound that distinguishes it no different than a finger print does each human being."

I could tell the mumbo-jumbo was inciting impatience for my father but he hadn't the heart to stop the master.

"I believe we'll soon be able to improve our players' plate output by training them to read the sonic print of the ball, and to *see* the ball as a type of hyperbolic expression. What I'm saying is—"

"Mr. Wolf, don't worry. None of us ever keep up," Sky

interrupted, assuming that it was her duty to translate. "If you'll allow me to interpret, Whitman is saying that we can handle the rest of this."

"Mr. Wolf, my world is academic. But I'm still going to put baseball on a new orbit by next year."

"Good to hear, Whit. But until then use your bare knuckles, lad."

"Thanks, dad," I mentioned as we were near leaving. "There is one thing we didn't mention. There's a lot riding on us winning."

I handed him the agreement we had made with Thorne. He scanned it, his delight growing as he went through the pages.

"Any two players of his you want, for free! I guarantee you, once you beat him, his career in baseball is over."

"We could prosecute him for theft," Whitman suggested.

"Avoid the law. It's like an evil woman, costs a fortune and in the end it destroys you. Now get out there and win. Isn't this fun?"

As I've made clear, my dad was a one of a kind hand dealt from a stacked deck.

How was it possible that two men who had to share some genes from the same collection could approach life so differently? He would have stared down a dragon and if shown disrespect spit back in its face. He vowed to me that he never showed temerity when dealing with the ladies, at least until he met my mom. (She changed the game by promising to castrate him if he proved un-faithful…she had to have given him an earnest shiver when she laid down her law because I'm certain he's been as devoted to her as a worker bee to the queen.)

Yet as much a near mythological figure as he was, his son was cowering from the thought of asking the last person on earth that would want to hurt him for a night out together. I guess I was as wild a card as he; I hadn't yet learned to fix the game in my favor.

During the meeting with my father, I watched Sky. Her only concern was how she was going to win. It was a code of honor for her, an indestructible element defin-ing who she was, whom she had no choice other than to be. I could see the admiration in my father's face, a growing respect she appeared oblivious to.

More and more, I witnessed the similarities in their character and person, and I found my love for each of them growing greater and greater. I knew my father adored me in return. Sky? I couldn't imagine her lusting for me.

Several times while with my father that afternoon, I looked at her and as many times she willingly made eye contact with me. Rather than letting the sign serve to encourage me, I reduced it to a polite gesture. Still, I wanted her, more than anything in the world.

CHAPTER 17: LET'S MAKE A DEAL

What came off as surreal was in fact a meeting with representatives of each of the major league franchises. On two of the walls of the large convention room were giant bulletin boards covered with over-sized-charts that appeared to be dotted randomly with large red, green, yellow and blue pins. At the front of the room was a long table with a microphone in front of a seated man. Behind him, elevated half way to the ceiling was a banner stretching across most of the room. It read: ANNUAL BASEBALL TRADE DEADLINE MEETING.

Then off to the right was a giant wheel, in fact a replica of a wheel of fortune found in most every gambling establishment in the world. The room was filled with tables; the centerpieces were composed of artfully crafted baseball gloves with a single bat rising upward out of each with a sign attached, signifying the name of the team assigned to each one. The tables all had several people sitting around whispering, and there were even more of the men scattered about the room chatting with one another.

We had been assigned a location off to the corner. It reminded me of where a restaurant might want to seat a family with an infant so as to not disturb the other guests. Sky was seated alone at our table, being ignored by the rest of the executives.

Music began playing to announce the opening of the event. Six stunning young ladies entered the room from each side and stood in front of the elongated table. They were wearing fashionable baseball uniforms composed of caps, sexy tops and skirts. Around each of their waists was a belt that held a baseball glove on one side and a small bat on the other. Their role was to put on a dance routine choreographed to the music. When they completed the opening scene, the man seated at the front of the room stood up.

"How's that for baseball's first even Trade Deadline meeting?" He smiled invitingly, gaining the response he was employed to achieve.

The crowd roared their appreciation, clapping and cheering, gawking at the collection of sensual ladies. Then one of the girls went to the right side of the room and stood beside the bulletin boards. After a moment the announcer motioned to her. Then, on cue she scampered over to hand him a piece of paper. He scanned it and whispered to the lady, who then took the paper and went back to stand by the board.

"Opening bid on Kavenaugh is a hundred grand," he paused to clear his throat, "plus a triple-AAA prospect. Let's get those check books out fellows."

The audience seemed to pay little attention but after a few seconds a voice shot out from the table with the Indians' flag.

"We'll take it, Mike."

"One ten," countered a voice from the Mariners' headquarters.

Then the room went silent again. The auctioneer tried to rouse the bidders.

"Fellows, he's a fine talent. Is that all I'm going to get? That's it. Going once." He intentionally hesitated. "Going twice." This time he waited a few seconds longer. "Gone to the Mariners."

A few more rounds followed, none of the pieces of merchandise inspiring much excitement up to that point.

It was well into the process when Karlov showed up. He rushed into the room, short of breath as he reached the table where Sky was still seated alone. He was wearing a hip bright orange-colored, eye-catching suit and he had his hair trimmed, now worn in a spiked style. He had transformed his appearance, now looking more like a hustler than a business executive.

"I said I'd take you shopping," Sky squinted, not believing what he had done to himself.

"There's this cool store near my house. That's why I'm late; they forgot to press the suit."

"Professor, did you tell the salesman what sort of work you're doing?"

"No. Why?"

"They may have thought you're a pimp," Sky commented, but without even a hint of humor.

"But do I look okay?" Karlov asked childishly.

"Next time can I go clothes hunting with you?" Sky cleverly avoided answering.

"Where are Ben and Whitman?"

"There are some changes I'll have to tell you about."

"What?"

"Ben and Whitman are both leaving the team," Sky disclosed.

"I'm not shocked "Karlov answered.

"To be honest, it's not their thing. They both have other interests but I'll let Ben tell you himself when he gets here. Whitman, I'm sure you can figure it out, is going to do research. He believes he's on the cutting edge of revolutionary work that will change sports for decades to come. Needless to say, he'll stay on as a consultant only."

"That kid will do whatever he envisions. I knew that the first time I had him in class," Karlov complimented.

"Ben, Whitman and I came into this together and we've talked a lot about what each of us wants to achieve professionally," Sky related. She then looked discerningly at Karlov. "The bottom line is, professor, that it's just you and I now."

"Me? Like what do you have in mind?"

"Well, I'm offering for you to be my assistant."

"What are you talking about?"

"Mr. Wolf invited me to stay on as GM…it's simple, I need someone I can trust to back me up."

"Well…um…I'm shocked but…absolutely." Karlov seemed confused. "Why are you staying? You're a young lady with a future in your field; this is a man's world and they'll never respect you."

"I don't need them to respect me. Besides, it's not a man's world now, is it? How long do you think it'll be before a pro hockey team, a basketball or football franchise, finds the right leader in a female body?" Sky posed. "And I'll tell you something else. To be honest, before the season began I'd never in my life been to a baseball game. My plan was to be a mathematician. But I've fallen in love with baseball."

"It can get under your skin. Here I am, revered in my field and all I ever dreamed of was the opportunity you're offering me. There's something magical about the game."

"I know. Karlov, I love the wisdom. I love the spiting and spitting. I love the hate and I love the love. I love the spirit, the roar of the crowd, the precision and the pure mathematics in every pitch and every stroke of the bat...but most of all, you know what I love?" she asked as if mystified.

"You're doing well. I'm waiting,"

"I love the tradition. Baseball is as big as life; that's why it is America's game as much as a burger and apple pie is our national food."

"Boss, you're starting to sound like me, a true believer," Karlov joked.

Karlov couldn't resist a drink. From inside his coat pocket he took a flask and poured an amber substance in a glass. One of the waitresses who had served as a dancer at the start of the event noticed and came rushing over to the table.

"Sir, I can get you anything you want," she offered in a most provocative tone.

"Two Jims, coke on the side," Karlov ordered.

The lovely lady scurried off with the order. Just seconds later, Whitman and I arrived. I had been working on a side project and came in proudly hoisting a document for both of them to see.

"Deal sealed," I heralded. "Let me read. Yes, this is the meat of it. Capital Entertainment guarantees... blah, blah, blah...millions, yes millions, per year for the next five years for the exclusive rights to license Magic Music."

"Blah, blah, blah millions? I guess we're all rich," Sky giddily concluded.

"We're richer than rich. By Whitman's calculations we'll triple the guaranteed amount."

"At least," Whitman exalted. "Everything will be out in the open. The patent will hold up and they'll be using it only toward human growth and scientific healing—we control content."

"Whit, do they know that Thorne and us have used it? Sky questioned.

"They could care less." Whitman assured her. "I'm not finished. I'll have my next generation of aids for athletes ready for testing within months. I promise, Sky, they're yours exclusively for the first few years," he offered magnanimously. "And by the way, congratulations, professor."

"I think your new job should solve all of your problems," I added.

"I can't even tell you fellows how excited I am."

"You'll do great," I assured him.

I watched as Sky pushed back her chair and reached under the table. Her right hand came out holding what I recognized was a violin case. She placed it in front of me.

"Thought you might like a new one," she smiled.

As I opened it, I was staring at the exact instrument I had been considering buying.

"How did you know I wanted this one?"

"I know a lot of things," she said mysteriously.

At that moment, all the tension between us dissolved. It was as if it had never been there, the two of us as peaceful with one another as we'd ever been in the past. I thought it would be wonderful to leave it at that, grateful that we were still friends bonded for life—I knew I'd never be able to do that. I loved Sky.

I still had no plan for pursuing my passion but I saw for the first time in her eyes what I would have bet meant that she had a similar feeling for me.

"Sky, this costs—"

"Shush. Not now. Make beautiful music with it and it will be worth every penny of the fortune you just told me I'll have."

"You're leaving too, Ben. 'Like father, like son'—didn't work for you?" Karlov politely injected.

"It just never seemed right."

Karlov leaned close to me, his small eyes speaking lamentation. "My father was a Major General in the marines. It didn't work for me either."

Karlov's father was a Major General in the U. S. Marines. I knew Whitman's father was a mason, but had birthed a neurokinetic freak for a son. It made no sense to me. Arnold Wolf, one of the greatest industrialists in American history, fathered a classical musical composer with as much business savvy as a terrorist: that made no sense to me either.

How comical, I thought. Here was Karlov and I, two misfits who had spent likely years of our lives trying to reconcile who we were by measuring ourselves against our fathers, without ever considering that perhaps those men might have spent the same years trying to reconcile who they were by measuring themselves against their sons.

Will the real set of misfits please stand up? I laughed. In my make-believe television program, nobody rose. It was all in our respective imaginations. I laughed again. How foolish we are as human beings, suffering to find ourselves in the image of another, failing to inspect from within where all the answers are beckoning us to take them at any moment we wished.

Then I glanced once more at Sky. Was I doing the same thing, looking for her to answer my puzzle? Could the source of my cowardliness be that I needed her to signal to me that it was safe to approach and that I wouldn't be rejected as opposed to me resolving for myself what my feelings were before acting on them? In other words, if I were so confident in my passion for her then what would be inhibiting me from bringing my love to her?

I quickly recognized that facing the inner self might be an act of greater heroism than even what I perceived was required to approach Sky. I had work to do and might have taken another step or two right then, had I not been interrupted.

"Time for the 'A' class players, folks" the announcer called out. "This is where the top of the line talent, the potential All-Stars and Hall of Famers, are one bid away from playing for your team."

One of the girls showed off her charm as she traipsed across the room and up to the wheel. She used her hand to set it spinning.

"Gentlemen, we'll be selecting the order of the players available by spinning the dial. Remember, minimum bids apply."

The same girl spun the wheel a second time and backed away waiting for it to stop on a name.

"Pappas, New York, second base," she called out after reading the wheel.

The level of enthusiasm rose discernibly as the upper echelon players came up for bids. By now the room was buzzing with discussion.

"Forget these guys," Karlov instructed Sky, "I have my eyes set on Wilcox."

"Why Wilcox?" Sky wondered out loud. "We never discussed him before."

"A little secret," Karlov proudly announced. "Best *Holy Shit* hitter in baseball."

"What is a Holy Shit hitter, may I ask," Sky queried.

"He's the guy that makes every pitcher say 'Holy Shit' when they have to pitch to him."

"Karlov, I never saw his name on the trade roster, come to think of it," Sky deliberated. "I don't think Wilcox is available."

"Pocket listing; he's meat on the block."

What was hysterical was that for each of the players up for sale, there was a life-size blow-up replica. When their name came up on the wheel, the likeness of that fellow dropped out of the ceiling, which was covered by a thin tarp. Then after it was released to floor level, one of the ladies unhooked it and paraded it around the room like a specimen at a hog auction: it wasn't flattering and I wondered how these men would feel watching themselves being treated like cattle.

"Thanks, doll," Karlov smiled as the same girl dropped off his drinks.

She was ready to leave when he called for her attention. "Wait." He then whispered in her ear.

The three of us looked, noticing she nodded her head in an agreeable gesture. After she left, we waited with eager anticipation for him to explain what happened but he said nothing.

"Well?" Sky finally asked.

"Well, what?"

Karlov couldn't hold his elation back any longer.

"She said she'd go out with me tonight."

Each one of us congratulated him with slaps on the back and high-fives.

"Baseball. Women. My life has definitely turned."

"It's got to be the suit," Sky teased.

"There is the man who has the rights to Wilcox," Karlov nodded to point out across the room where Ted Simon of The White Sox was sitting. "I think you should make the first contact, Sky."

Sky stood up and went over to him. She voiced her words softly and he responded. After a moment, she came back to our table.

"You were right. Simon was instructed by his owner to peddle Wilcox," she informed Karlov. "Only one problem. He's already got a deal for him."

"It's the Angels," Karlov filled in. "They're desperate for a heavy bat."

"If you know all this, then why send me on a mission I can't accomplish?" Sky asked.

"Because the trade is not completed. Plus, The Angels need a long-term contract. You see, Wilcox is going to be a very pricey commodity at the end of the year when he declares free agency."

"Wait a second," Sky reasoned. "If I'm reading you right, you're thinking that our need is immediate but ends after the season. By then, after we've whipped Thorne, we'll be able to load up our roster with his best jewels."

"Right. And in the meantime we—"

"No wonder you're the professor," Sky complimented her new assistant. "In the meantime, we find a replacement for The Angels that they can afford long-term and who is a damn good player as well—just not up to Wilcox' stature. Whitman, who's out there?"

Whitman pulled out a list but before he could scan it, Karlov stopped him.

"Forget it, Whitman. There's only one guy who fits the bill and that's Carson from Kansas City. He's too expensive for The Royals to keep but he's got another five years left on his contract."

"So, first we give Bob Wyatt of Kansas City a deal he can't afford to refuse," Sky pronounced like a verdict. "Then we go to Andy Houston of The Angels and he'll be thrilled that he's got a player he can count on for years."

"Sounds good," Karlov concurred. "You just have to pull it off."

"Oh, no. That's your job, buddy."

"Then I guess I'm going to Kansas City...and then to Los Angeles to meet with The Angels. Wish me luck."

"I remember somebody saying there was very little of it in baseball," I bantered at Karlov.

"Very funny. That was before I was a baseball exec."

Karlov left on his mission, Sky gloating over the situation.

"Guys, this is win-win, except for Simon, of course. If his owner is insisting he get rid of Wilcox, he has only until the end of the meeting today to do it and soon we'll be his only bidder—who the hell will be willing to pay anything for a player who is going to put themselves out for sale in a few months? We're going to rape Simon," she declared deliciously.

"Rape. What's a nice girl like you talking like that for?" Whitman picked up on Sky's lust for quoting Godfather film lines, sounding like an actor in the same movie.

We watched as Karlov made the rounds, moving repeatedly between Kansas City's table and The Angels'. While he was negotiating, Whitman seemed preoccupied with his computer. A moment later, another life-sized player replica was being exhibited in front of the teams.

It was Thorne who was up first, raising his team's flag.

"The Rivals offer full contract plus two triple-AAA players."

We listened as a couple other bids not exceeding his by much were placed. Then Thorne raised his flag again, taking the bidding a notch higher.

"Don't let Thorne have Carrillo," Whitman yelled. "He's a great first baseman."

"Remember what my dad said, Sky. Spend, spend, spend," I reminded her.

The auctioneer had gathered the bids but the room had been silent for several seconds after the last by Thorne.

"You're right, Ben. Wilcox and then Carrillo. Music or no music we'll clobber the schmuck for good," Sky agreed. "Ben, how about taking it as your last task as a co-GM for The Blue Stripes?"

"The Blue Stripes want to increase the last offer by two million," I voiced as I stood up.

I noticed Thorne glaring at me from across the room. The words of the announcer might have sounded like blows of a hammer to him.

"Ten seconds, folks. A star is being born…going…going…going…and…gone. Sold to The Blue Stripes."

Thorne sat down, never looking back at our table.

"Think about how pissed off Thorne must be now," Sky rejoiced.

"Watching you, I think my dad may have been off a bit when he defined success entirely in terms of making money."

"What do you mean, Ben?"

"The way you put yourself into what you do…you become the absolute best at it. You really love it; that's success."

"That's what your dad said," she responded matter-a-fact.

"That's what he said? Not to me. To me it was about making money."

"You have to listen more carefully, darling. Making money and achieving success are one and the same."

I leaned back in my chair, appreciating her wisdom, knowing it was right for her, right for my father, but accepting that it didn't have to be right for me. She was the female version of my dad, no doubt about it. Sky had found her groove. She was destined to leave her mark in the game of baseball, and doing so in indelible ink.

What was I going to do, not about the game of baseball but the game of romance? As had always been the case, I had no answer. Yet as I deliberated, unexpectedly I noticed a peaceful sensation envelop me. Then it turned to a warm gentle breeze, and it started blowing, charging my floppy sails with willful command. I could feel the mouth of destiny whistling and its lips about to kiss me tenderly as it set my ship to sea, to journey to new lands where I'd be a conqueror of my dream of castles in my sky. Could I be vanquished, turned away at the gates of love, suffering for the caress I now believed essential for me to breath, taste, see and feel?

The transient tranquility I had enjoyed was a sign; it was time to get down to business with the lady I sat next to.

"Sky, there's something I've wanted to discuss with you."

"You told me that once before but you never followed up on it," she poked playfully but with a bit of admonishment evident in her voice.

"I wasn't ready."

"When will you be ready, Ben?"

My father never had much faith in destiny. Luck? You could count on it about as much as a promise before an orgasm. Then what was it that kept sticking its tongue out at me every time I was on the verge of laying my heart at her feet? It was Thorne this time.

Yes. Yes. Yes. At that imperfect instant, Thorne was on his way toward us, intentionally selecting an exit door close to our table. As he approached he stopped, timing his words precisely so as to interrupt me.

"I thought you had no money?" he questioned condescendingly.

"We found a friendly bank," Sky chirped.

"I'll bet."

Thorne left without another word, his wrath enough to veer my pubescent craft off course and to permit the middle finger of fate to point at me.

"I can't quite explain it," Whitman jived, "but there is something I don't like about that guy."

I can't say if my sweet damsel had been equally thrust off track by Thorne's foul intrusion but she addressed Whitman's remark with a full release of laughter—had she wiggled out of my psychological grip intentionally or was it not meant to be that I man up my heart? I wouldn't find out right then. The return of Karlov settled my fortunes, at least for the moment.

Come on. Guts and will are conditions we all need at times. But what about a plain, pure white break; shouldn't each of us be entitled to fortuity's favor at least once in a while? Sadly, it wasn't going to be my once in that while.

"Andy Houston is ecstatic. Kansas City is relieved

and…Wilcox is definitely in our back pocket," Karlov trumpeted his great accomplishment.

Sky was back to work, leaving me deflated. She motioned to one of the waitresses to come to her. Then she whispered something to the girl. I watched the messenger walk over to Ted Simon and give him a verbal note. Simon said a few words to one of the other men at his table and then came to speak to Sky.

"You mentioned you had an offer for Wilcox." Sky informed him of a fact he'd never disclosed to her; she was so convincing he assumed he had.

"What about it?"

"I don't suspect it's from Andy Houston of The Angels?"

"Ms…"

"Mills. My full name is Skyler."

"Well, Ms. Mills," Simon patronized. "Matter-a-fact it is."

"You may want to check with him before you get too comfortable. We just made a deal for Carson. He's on his way to the Angels."

"I don't understand," Simon answered, seemingly ruffled. "I thought—"

"Houston's right over there; you can ask him yourself."

Simon did. We observed his face droop as the conversation ensued. By the time he came back to our table, he might have been suffering food poisoning.

"Son of a bitch. This is not the way we had it worked out."

"Deals don't always come out the way we expect," Sky sympathized with an equally condescending voice. "Look, we're still interested in Wilcox. Sure, he's only good for a short spurt to the finish, but we're willing to assume future risk."

"I'm not giving him away," Simon asserted, though his words sounded closer to a plea.

"You don't have to," Karlov inserted. "But you know as well as I do that you'll have to come up with a minimum of eighty million to sign him after the end of the season. Your boss isn't going to ante up, especially with you so far from playoff contention you wouldn't get there if you won every game from here on. You need to boot him before the deadline ends and that's about an hour from now. You never officially listed him so unless you can scamper around this room and find someone else willing to take him, you're going home to an angry owner."

"Mr. Simon, you're not about to face that, are you?" Sky reinforced her partner's argument.

"Well, I'll admit we don't have that kind of money to commit right now."

"Then it's settled. We'll take Simon off your hands and in exchange...professor we need two prime prospects to award Mr. Simon so he doesn't have to go home to a spanking," Sky said gaily. "Come on, what do we have to offer in exchange?"

"Harper and Enriquez?"

"Sounds good to me," Sky swooned. "So if you'll also assume the rest of the year's salary for Wilcox we have a deal."

Simon was clenching his jaw. I thought I saw his hands shaking, the urge to strangle my lover had to be nearly indomitable. He dolefully walked off, fortunately without first assaulting her.

"What can I say, guys," Whitman chanted. "Just another happy day, another date with Merci, another merci," he accented in French. "Oh, have mercy on me. Catch you up before sup."

Whitman had officially retired from his role as co-GM, no wonder. During the following weeks he'd be busy shuffling his amour between Merci, Kona and a few other sweethearts he'd be caressing. Haunting him for years, he was finally achieving his potential as a stud.

Still, in his own way, he had been bit by the sport's bug to the extent he became infatuated with finding novel methods to improve an athlete's output. Sure, he was ecstatic about having his choice of lady friend, but equally important to him was that his research was proving to be every bit as successful as he promised. Then just as Whitman's direct role with The Blue Stripes was winding down, Karlov's was gloriously revving up.

"Is there anything else for me to do here?" Karlov posed to Sky.

"Not a thing really. But if you want to go back to your new office, it's on the fifteenth floor, right next to mine." Sky enthralled him. "Oh, by the way, your secretary, Yvette, is waiting for you."

Karlov was beaming. He stood to leave, with Whitman accompanying him out of the room. That left Sky and me alone. She lifted her head and made no apology as her eyes journeyed uninhibited to visit mine. Her breathing was steady but deeper than normal and I might have sworn that in addition to the remnants of the old Sky, the girl who loved to tease and giggle, I perceived a faint blushing of her skin around the neck and upper portion of her chest, the shyness of a virgin's willful submission.

"Well, what is it you wanted to talk about?"

"Us."

Fear's an enemy to action, no doubt. It can talk a person out of even the most elemental advantageous or life-giving opportunity. It can demoralize courage and stagnate the senses. It can ravage passion and declare victory over human will. It can put a bullet through the eye of a dream.

Yet the functions performed by this most reviled emotion are not entirely damaging to members of our species. It can serve to alert the neural patterns of the mind that a pause can be life-saving. It can slow the organs of the body to provide that instant of time needed to defend against potentially mortal danger.

For me, at that moment with Sky, the anxiety I experienced served as a sword to slice the connective pathways between thought and action: the world all of a sudden stood still, in a condition of quiescence and motionlessness. It permitted me to let my single word travel the short distance between my senses and hers while I sat in the nothingness of…everything. *Us.* The word was better than syrup on pancakes.

She was the world to me, the totality of my universe. Making the experience even more special was that I was able to maintain the eye-to-eye contact with her, yet be awaiting nothing. I had no expectation or want; the state I found myself in transcended volition.

"What about us, Ben?" she drilled at me, puncturing my calm. "What about us?" she repeated but with less put-up-or-shut-up dare.

"I'm wondering if I'm still on that list," I released as unrehearsed as gas.

"What list?" she answered, deadpan.

"Whatever list it was that you said you had," referring to a conversation we had long before when she joked that she'd think about putting me on her list…whatever list it was.

Sky laughed awkwardly. "I'll have to double check but if I recall correctly you're still there."

"Well good…I think. Look, I have to say this. We're

friends for life but I want to take you out, just once, no labels attached…to see how it feels."

Sky stood up, leaning her hands on the table in front of her, still reading me with her wide-open hazel eyes while the pink flesh around her throat turned to flame red.

"Are you proposing a drink…or is this a full-on date?"

"A real date. The whole thing," I proposed as if I was handing her an engagement ring. "I pick you up, take you to a movie and out to eat, and then…" I rose from my chair to give myself a few inches advantage, "kiss you good-night if it goes well."

The fear hadn't abandoned me. This time it must have numbed me because she might have impaled me with a rejection spear and I'd have had no sensation of the stab or the life-blood draining from my system. I can't claim it was courage that had allowed me to place my heart in her possession to do with as she wished but I did it, that's all that counted to me.

"Hum, first you entice me to be a GM of a baseball team and my life changes. Now you want to romance me into a date…and god knows what then."

"You have to look past the silk suits and Italian shoes. I'm just an old-fashioned guy," I responded with the hope of bringing comic relief to the situation.

Then she shocked me. She waited some time and I could see she was handpicking her words. She wasn't smiling and there was nothing close to humor in the demeanor she exhibited. Instead, she appeared to be kowtowing to her own fear; she struck me as fragile, vulnerable and unsure of herself.

"I suppose I should have known this day would come," she finally murmured.

"It's a good day."

Then I did the unimaginable. I have no concept what was unfolding around me in the baseball trade meeting and I doubt Sky did either. It was one of those instances when the world is shut out and a bomb might explode but both you and your lover would be ignorant that the earth was shaking.

I made a journey—a hundred and eighty degrees, halfway around our table, the distance between one solar system and another, a trip that required no more than a fraction of a millionth of a second and no less than a billionth of eternity at the same time—I took her in my arms.

It was like soaring to the only cloud in the sky, enveloping myself in its warm softness while gently wrapping it in my embrace. I smelled what I wanted to believe was the thrill of her senses beckoning me, I fingered delicately strands of hair as fine as the sun's rays, I felt the heat of her skin warming to my touch, and saw as I voyaged into her eyes the loneliness I imagined only I owned.

"You won't regret it, Sky."

I'll cherish her reply for all of my life.

"That's what I'm worried about."

CHAPTER 18: GOOD AND BAD; INSEPARABLE BROTHERS

After the trade meeting, everything went along normally for a couple of weeks. Thorne's Rivals were continuing to win, closing the win-loss gap between our two teams. Then magically, their performance dropped off; they seemed to be the same mediocre team they had been before Thorne stole the music.

Several times during their downfall, I asked my father what he thought accounted for the dramatic change in output for the Rivals. On each occasion, he'd shake his head to suggest that it seemed like the strangest thing to him as well. But that was followed by a smirk that tattled on the fact that he knew exactly what had happened, and further that he was the mastermind behind the counter stealth operation that had destroyed the music files stolen by Thorne.

I was sure destruction is what had happened. I was certain that several weeks passed during which time Thorne's team was sinking in the standings. During that same span of time, my father had upped the level of security in the building. I should say that he employed real security. I was even more convinced that he'd had a hand in Thorne's decline, when during that period the sports' pages across the country were running stories about The Rivals' owner, Buck Stillwater, the CEO of Galactic Energy, unimaginably firing the esteemed Reed Thorne.

The buzz initially was that Thorne was going to land in Texas, California or Washington, D. C. Then, shortly thereafter, the nightly news was chattering about leaks suggesting that Thorne had somehow deceived Mr. Stillwater. The pundits surmised there could be no other explanation for the abrupt termination and the lack of offers from other organizations. The truth was that my father had a heart-to-heart with Buck and apprised him that The Rivals were about to take a worse bath than missing the playoffs, The Blue Stripes helping themselves to two of his prime players and costing him their millions in salary on top of the talent drain.

Thorne was finished in baseball. The other owners may not have felt endeared to my father but they surely respected him. Once the word spread that Thorne was a disreputable man, no team would lay a finger on him. As the senior Wolf stated in prose: *Not a person on this earth could ever make me feel the hurt that I command for any man who steals a dime from me. Felons heed my warning you will surely hear me roaring down your back with a dagger and a laugh."*

Thorne should have known better, but he was an arrogant type who thought he could beat the house. He was busted. The only person disappointed that his demise took place was Sky. By the time it was public record that he was a persona non grata, she was moaning that she never had the opportunity to derail him on her own terms. It continued to amaze me how similar she was to the old man.

Since we were into a full dating mode, I paid attention to her appetite for vengeance. Personal offenses were inconsequential to her but acts of dishonesty or disloyalty were never with impunity. I definitely would refrain from crossing her. Then again what was there to worry about, I loved her.

By then I was accustomed to the attention Sky commanded in public. Her name was as common in magazines and newspapers as any celebrity. She was invited to speak on talk shows, her face was routinely seen on the pages of the sport's section of our newspaper, and she had even appeared on the cover of Sports Illustrated. There was nowhere we went that people didn't stop to chat with her or ask for her autograph.

Surprisingly, the fame didn't seem to coat her with an air of conceit. As far as I could observe, she could have cared less. I do recall just prior to the season wrapping up—the team already preparing for the playoffs—an occasion when she appeared on RTN's Sports Page.

Dean Rockwell, the lead on the show, kindly introduced her as the, "Goddess of Baseball."

"Nobody can believe what you did with The Blue Stripes this year," Ms. Mills. "I know you've been asked too many times what you attribute the success to but I have to explore that point again."

"Me too," chimed in Chad DeWitt, another panelist. "You were doomed from the get-go, yet out of the fire of demise you rose like a phoenix? My lord, Sky, you've become a folk hero, a baseball legend in one season."

"I think I'm getting a tad more credit than I deserve. I had help all the way. Regarding your question of the team's unexpected positive performance, we knew the potential our players had and figured out a way to get them to play up to it."

"I think you're being modest, Sky, if you don't mind my saying it," offered Barry Borden, the third member of the show. "But I want to talk about something else with you. It's one thing putting together a winning team. You've done it and we here at Sports' Page take our hats off to you. But that's just the beginning. Do you realize that attendance this year is up seven percent over last year—that's for the entire league? Then on top of that, literally the entire growth is attributed to women following the sport and coming out to see a game."

"That's the problem with having had an exclusive

boy's club for so many years. As soon as a female member is admitted, she becomes a hero. I don't buy it. There are a hell of lot of other ladies out there that can lead as well as I can. I'm not trying to be humble, simply realistic. But no, women are not going to share the roster of teams in equal number to men athletes."

"Will they make it to the majors, in your opinion?" asked Rockwell.

"With rare, very rare exception." She stopped to deliberate, quickly correcting herself. "No, I doubt they ever will. Why compete where you'll lose. I'm not trying to bat a ball because my men can do that for the team. I'm there to make the deals, motivate the players, inspire the scouts, keep a budget and make sure the fans are properly rewarded for the money they're spending to support our team. I promise you, I'm a test case. Women will be doing what I do for many organizations in the very near future. Competing on the field with men? To do that competitively, they might have to be violating our substance programs," she quipped.

"On to the playoffs," Borden mentioned excitedly. "Will The Blue Stripes take it all the way this year, and if so, why?"

"We all know that lots of things can happen as the season nears the close. That said, if we stay healthy we have as good a chance as any team," she smiled mysteriously.

We didn't stay healthy.

We were closing out the season, when our fortunes

took a pair of hard turns—left and right. Israel Vargas, one of our starting left-handed pitchers tore his left rotator cuff and after medical examination was lost for the remainder of the year; we were informed that he had no choice but corrective surgery. Only two days later, Cory Kubiak, a right-hander who was considered the best pitcher on our staff and one of the top ten in the majors, was unimaginably assaulted at a convenience store he had stopped at on his way to the park. Most astonishing was that he had been clubbed with a steel pipe on his right shoulder, severely crushing the shoulder blade and eliminating any chance of him being available for the playoffs.

We had Magic Music but no Magic Medicine to remedy our bad luck.

Sky and I happened to be at the park taking in an afternoon game, when we were notified why Cory hadn't showed up on the day he was scheduled to pitch. After hearing the news at first, she didn't say a word. I knew what she was thinking, that we were past the deadline to alter our rotation through either trades or purchases. The only option was to pull up recruits from our farm system, a very risky proposition since even with our musical advantage, they were more inexperienced at post-season play than the lineup we were fielding—few of our prospect players had even been in a single major league game.

"I wonder," Sky sincerely deliberated. "Could they

switch arms? Vargas needs a left and Cory's is fine. Kubiak needs a right and Vargas' is in perfect working order."

"You better call Karlov and see if he has a number for that," I quipped.

What am I going to do? She mumbled as she took my hand in hers.

I was in heaven. She leaned her head on my shoulder and said nothing else. It was always the silence I experienced in her presence that thrilled me. By that point in our relationship, I'd come to trust that it was the same for her; for the remainder of the game she didn't mention either of the two injured players.

As we sat in the hush of our cocoon amidst the thundering and roaring of the enlivened crowd enjoying their Blue Stripes whipping The Rivals, I thought back on the long journey I'd traveled since the day I set eyes on Sky. I watched that first day at school as almost every male student's heart slipped a beat as she swished across the room. She appeared unfazed—better still, unaware—of their longing to gain her favor.

She smiled at each of them equally. The slight twitch of her neck as she encountered one after another was identical. She listened with the same degree of attentiveness as the line of males eager to take their turn talking with her paraded past.

I watched but didn't at the time possess sufficient courage to take my place in the hunt. I'm certain that had it not been for that bear that came within seconds of making a meal of each of us, I would have never made the connection with her I did. Then, had it not been for Thorne's deceit toward my father, it's not likely that we would have worked as intimately over so many months.

Grow up. Get some guts.

I could have shied away from the opportunities to engage her until finally she gave up and moved on to find a more likely prospect to play games of lust with the amorous feelings she had never expressed. But could I really have continued to behave as the coward I'd been up to then?

I realized I could not have. I had grown up...and along the way acquired guts—that was all she wanted from me, all she had been waiting for. It may have been the ultimate goal my father had from the beginning, simply to see me come alive, to witness the passion in my soul, "spend a summer of Sundays in ripped of shoes, making love in the afternoons, while nothing in the world could hurt me."

It was a fact that finding the love of my life had set my musical expressions to new heights. I had always been talented. Often my instructors would complement me on my potential as an artist. But what I didn't realize was that at the same time they were praising me, they were criticizing my lack of determination...chastising me for being short of daring to make myself the best I could be.

As we sat with our hands clasping one another and

her head on my shoulder, I turned to look at her. I faintly heard the cheers of the thousands of Blue Stripe devotees as Wilcox earned a solid "Holy Shit" from The Rivals' pitcher who watched as the ball soared over the left field wall. She never gazed out at the plate. Instead she stared back at me and smiled.

"I'll never let go of you," I shouted over the din of the crowd.

"No. I'll never let go of you," she spoke for only me to hear.

Guts can take you a long way. Mine took its sweet time ripening but as they say, better late than never.

CHAPTER 19: THE GREATEST WORLD SERIES EVER

The Blue Stripes might have been a collection of transplants from Krypton, a team of Superman characters mercilessly overmastering the playoff competition right up to the World Series. Even short our two top pitchers, we miraculously tamed our most able foes.

We had Magic Music playing in the locker room, in the gym, on every recording device owned by one of our players, on the field during the warm ups and even in the player's bathroom—for all I know, Sky had it snuck into the players' homes. We were infusing them with more enhancements than the Roadrunner computer; these men were on audio steroids.

Still, Sky wasn't the least bit overconfident. I noticed her tensing up as the few days passed leading up to the big series. Karlov, on the other hand, was in heaven; he'd follow Sky like a frisky puppy dog. He had little to do at that point in terms of formal duties but took it upon himself to re-assure Sky that The Blue Stripes, even short two starting pitchers, were a shoe-in to take first prize.

I watched the show unfolding. My father took a passive role too. Each game he'd show up and observe from the opening pitch to the last out, yet he never intervened by offering advice to Sky. I could tell that he was concerned about her because whenever I'd speak with him, he'd ask me how she was holding up. He was well aware of the fact that we had taken a beating in terms of losing two pitchers so late in the season, and that we should have been eliminated. Yet there we were, swishing our magic swords to vanquish our enemies.

The beginning of The Series didn't go well. We still had two outstanding arms in our pitching rotation, Rudy Petrofsky and Mika Flores. However, being concerned that we could get eliminated early, our manager, Leo Durham, saw no choice but to risk using the twosome as much as he possibly could. They had held up remarkably well. But then the probability that nobody wanted to admit—the least willing to do so the two pitchers themselves—happened.

Petrofsky was on the mound for the opening game and lasted all of two and a third innings before he was shelled. Down eleven to zip, at that point we hadn't a prayer of winning the first game. The next afternoon, Flores swore he felt better than ever. He ran onto the field like a rookie, kicking the back of his heel on the pitcher's plate, cleaning the small elevated area of the infield he would be calling home for as long as he could overpower the opposing players, and warming up by hurling balls that looked like cannon shots.

Thankfully, we could count on Flores to even the series. Well, at least he convinced everyone he would do it. He lasted exactly two innings, Durham yanking him after giving up eight runs and eleven hits—there was no music to ease this pain. The invincible Blue Stripes had lost the first two games. We were now coming home for the next three but with no choice other than to start two of those contests with pitchers as reliable as treating kidney cancer with purified water.

We were finished. The luck of The Blue Stripes had finally run out. That was the prevailing view of the pundits who nightly trashed our team and took delight expressing their view that we were playing way over our heads from the start and it was only a matter of time before we plopped down to earth.

Wrong. They may have believed that we were a crew of misfits and amateurs who were destined for failure but they were mistaken. By then, we had heart, and our boys had bonded like cement. They still believed in themselves and if nobody else did, it didn't matter to them. They were convinced they were going to prevail— and they did.

We took all three games on our home turf. The two

replacement pitchers we plucked from our AAA Magnets in Toledo, Ohio were indomitable. They worked the opposing hitters so brilliantly that both of their games ended in shutouts and the third game ended with a six to one victory.

Sure, we had the burden of playing the last two games in enemy territory but luckily their park was less than a hundred miles away, and the best news was that we were up one game with two to go. All we had to do was pray that Petrofsky and Flores had recovered psychologically from the beatings they took—and they had.

In the first game, Petrofsky gave up only three hits in seven innings and our relief staff completed two more hitless innings. We, contrary to their lame hitters, hammered their pitchers for fourteen hits and two walks in those same nine innings, but were unable to produce a single run.

As she sat next to me watching the game, Sky appeared to be ten years older than when the series began. She had no control over the events taking place on the field, yet she urgently wanted the win. All during the game, she nibbled on her fingernails, a habit I had witnessed on her part when under pressure. As the game neared the finale, she'd run out of surfaces to chomp down on. Kindly I slid my hand across to her and placed one of my fingers close to her mouth.

"What are you doing?" she snapped.

"I thought I'd offer you mine before you start eating your flesh."

"Ben, this isn't a joke," she grimaced before ranting on about the urgency of the situation. "We need to finish them off right here and now. Flores' great but he's tired. I'll have a talk with Durham if this goes to a seventh. He'll have a better chance putting Hitchcock out there or—"

"Sky, this one's not even over. Let's wait—"

My words were timed perfectly to the moaning and wailing of the crowd as our pitcher gave up a home run to the first hitter in the bottom half of the tenth inning.

"God damn it," Sky spit under her breath, never moving a muscle in her mouth. (She was aware that often the cameras would zero in on her to catch her reaction, especially at such a critical moment.) "Shit. I knew it, Ben. This thing was destined for seven from the beginning."

She was right—it was a terminal home run.

What was amazing about the series was that after the trouncing we took during the first two games, the pitchers had taken over and all the scores were extremely low thereafter; the hitters might have been on holiday.

Game seven was no different. Flores, contrary to Sky's prediction, was untouchable—unfortunately so was the opposing pitcher. It was a one to one tie going into the seventh inning stretch and the score was still unchanged beginning the ninth inning. The announcers were already labeling it the most exciting series in the history of baseball, and they may have been correct. Occasionally a hitter would reach first base, but rarely second. There were few errors; the fielding was remarkable and accounted for saving several runs on both sides.

Flores was taken out of the game for a pinch hitter as we came up to bat in the top of the ninth. Our team was definitely not making music because they went down in order; one, two, three, and we were in the bottom half of the inning.

"We had them yesterday. For Christ sakes, Karlov was so hot on Wilcox but where has his bat been all this time?" Sky griped.

"I've got my fingers crossed," I said as I held my hands out for her to inspect. "My toes are working too."

"This is not about luck, Ben. It's about guts and determination. That's is what this game comes down to."

There might be a Book of Excuses out there but Skylar Mills was not going to be quoted.

I watched as our best reliever, Wally Overton, warmed up for the bottom half of the inning. After ten pitches, he waved to the umpire that he was ready to work. Indeed, he was. His velocity was so high you could see fire around the perimeter of the ball as he launched it like a torpedo. Each throw varied in that one dropped as it neared the plate, another curved just as the batter swung at it, and another zoomed past before the hitter could get around on it—he struck out the first two men on a total of only eight pitches.

As our team had done the inning before, a pinch hitter was brought in for their pitcher. We breathed a sense of relief knowing that we were going for a tenth inning in that the joker they brought in to hit for the pitcher had a deplorable on-base percentage.

On the first pitch, Overton brushed him back with an inside fastball. But rather than pulling away from the bullet, the batter made a slight flinch, far from enough to get out of the way of the ball; he ended up taking the force of the ball on the fleshy part of his left shoulder.

It was obvious to our manager and players that he'd intentionally "taken one for the team," an act that if discerned by the umpire to have happened would result in him being called back to the batter's box rather than taking the free pass to first base.

As soon as the batter groaned and grabbed his arm, the umpire waved him to first and the player trotted like an injured brat. I thought I witnessed a smirk on his face as he glanced toward Overton, believing he'd made a fool of him.

It took only a fraction of a second for pandemonium to break out in the stadium. Because of the close proximity of our team to our opponents, the park was stuffed with a huge number of our fans. This was great for our morale but a potentially explosive formula under the circumstances.

Durham, our manager, a pudgy elderly man who epitomized everything non-athletic, raced to the plate as if he were a pregnant track star. He furiously confronted the home plate umpire, shouting invectives before he ever had a chance to hear from the field boss.

As he carried on, the opposing manager came to join in the circus. In fact, both benches were emptied. I was sure we were headed for a riot. Overton, a burly brute who stood five inches over six foot and had the build of a weight lifter, had dashed toward the much smaller batter now standing smugly on the first base pad. As soon as he noticed Overton, however, quickly closing the distance between them he headed for the safety of his dugout.

Three of our players were holding back Overton; it was a good thing because I have no doubt he'd have ended the man's career. Durham was furiously waving his arms, his belly popping forward like a Santa on a rampage. There was nothing to hear other than stomping, pounding and screeching of thousands of fans—there was security but not a full infantry, which is what would have been needed to subdue this hostile mob.

Luckily, Mayor Tollini was up above in a box with my father. It astonished me that he'd have the nerve to do it but he came down and walked on to the field, waving his arms in a gesture of calming, encouraging our fans to pipe down and let the baseball umpires pass a verdict on the situation.

Surprisingly, his intervention helped. After only about fifteen minutes, there was relative silence, enough that at least the voice of the announcer could be heard. By then all the umpires had huddled away from the influence of the managers to decide how to fairly intervene.

Finally, it was apparent they had reached a decision. You might have thought it was a football game, the head umpire doing the unprecedented action of using the public address system to announce their joint decision.

"We're asking you to behave like the proud baseball fans you are. We've considered the situation from each of our vantage points and collectively concur that the batter was hit by a pitch and will take first base."

It was controlled chaos. The home crowd was delirious and our visiting fans, still in the minority, wisely seemed to be keeping their mouths shut. It was no joke. The place might have turned to a battlefield. In fact, I tried to get Sky to come with me to a secured area but she refused.

She'd read every rulebook printed on major league baseball and knew that it was the umpires' discretion whether or not the batter intentionally took the hit; further she understood that it was a rarity that the batter was called back after the ball struck him.

Thankfully, the outrage had quieted down—too bad it wouldn't last.

Overton remained on the mound, taking several warm up pitches to get ready to finish off the inning. He stared down the batter from his stretch position and then glanced hatefully toward the player taking a large lead from first base. Then, as he was about to make his delivery, he rocketed the ball to first base in an attempt to pick off the runner. But instead of dashing back to the bag, the base runner took off toward second, sliding safely under the throw that came late from the first baseman.

Now there was a runner in scoring position with two outs. Overton went to work, quickly shooting two strikes past the batter. We were one single strike away from continuing our quest to win, a lone pitch separating us from hope.

Overton still pitched from the stretch. He aimed a fastball perfectly on the outside corner of the plate. The batter, reaching with the bat, was thrown off balance and ended up swinging sloppily at the ball. He hardly made contact. Still, he produced a loping fly ball headed benignly toward our outfielder, Wilcox.

It was a routine play. I took a quick peek at Sky, noticing an exhalation of relief—we were safely out of a jam. Wilcox was jogging to get under the high ball, holding out his glove. Then as he was about to get in position for the catch, the unimaginable happened.

A rat, a fat black specimen, was sprinting across the outfield, headed in Wilcox' direction. He must have sensed it close to him, because for an instant he took his eye off the ball. It was then he definitively noticed the rodent nearly under his feet. A look not suggesting astonishment but rather terror was evident on his face as his body lurched sideways to avoid a direct encounter with the beast, causing him to trip over his own foot, falling unceremoniously on the ground.

The ball dropped not five feet from him. By the time one of the other players reached where it laid inertly, it was over. The runner who had taken a hit for his team had already crossed the plate and was standing majestically as The World Series tragically ended for The Blue Stripes.

Sky looked shell-shocked.

Thousands of fans were now protesting the loss. It all came down to what, a batter cheating and a subsequent improbable event leading to him scoring when his team should have been headed toward further warfare with their competitor?

The clamor around us was deafening and threatening. I grabbed Sky by the arm and forced her through a narrow passageway adjacent to our box that led to the inner bowels of the stadium where we were ushered directly to the visitors' locker room.

Safe from the potential violence an angry crowd can cause, I took a deep breath of relief. As we stood alone awaiting our players, Sky took me in her arms and embraced me. She looked up at me and smiled.

"You know, Ben, we'll be together no matter what."

"I know. We will, and every year you'll have a new collection of players to win championships."

"Sure, next year I'll do it."

"Look what you did this year and you didn't even know the game going into spring training," I reminded her.

"It's amazing how Whitman is coming up with all the acoustical research on ball movement. Our boys are going to be in for a surprise when we begin training," Sky said enthusiastically.

She had no appetite for dwelling on the past. While she would have never expressed the glee that Thorne had at losing, she wasn't about to slump into a long state of gloom either.

Neither of us was looking forward to the players coming in. We knew what we were in store for but before that we unexpectedly had another surprise to deal with. My dad was making his way into the room. He didn't look pleased. We didn't know it but he was toting a load of controversy potentially more lethal than what might have happened in the stands.

CHAPTER 20: THE FINALE

Whitman and Karlov joined Sky and me just as my father strode in another door off to the side of the room. As he did, he motioned for us to follow him, leading us into a small office where we could talk privately.

"I thought I might brief all of you on what's coming up. I spent the last half hour with Kimmel, our esteemed commissioner. It seems some meddling S.O.B.," he paused to let us absorb the obvious reference to Thorne, "has suggested we unfairly competed this year and has alerted Kimmel that we have a secret weapon as scandalous as any illegal enhanced substance."

"But we didn't do anything to break laws. We were only—"

"Sky, dear, this is politics. I'm going to help you out here until you learn the ropes. We have the power to pop a cherry bigger than a celebrity virgin's. If we choose to wield it, baseball is going to be in a quandary. The commissioner already viewed the tape of that little caper pulled off today. The film shows indisputably that he took the pitch on his arm intentionally; he knows their manager was authorized to do it by Leiber, their owner. It's not like fixing The World Series but it is cheating."

"I was going to ask you about it. I've already been considering a first ever World Series protest and—"

"Stop right there," my father instructed Sky. "You sock me in the belly and I poke you in the eye. After a while your eye heals and my gut is normal in a half hour; we go on our separate ways. But if you shoot me in the chest and I take a two-by-four and club you over the head we don't heal so quickly, maybe never. Get the point?"

"We're the only ones who can challenge the call of the umpires and Kimmel is the only one who can launch a full investigation into our Magic Music," Whitman answered for Sky.

"Right. Our team will be made to look like swindlers; every one of our players' reputations will be depreciated. Baseball will be in an unprecedented dilemma over what to do about The World Series and how to clean up a public relations mess," Sky completed the line of reasoning that my father was metaphorically addressing.

"You're the GM, Sky. I'll leave it up to you how you want to handle it. You have my promise that I'll back you with everything I have, if you conclude in your heart that the right path is to protest."

"Thank you, sir. I really don't need time. I'd never harm this game," she said solemnly. "Besides," she beamed, "we believe we have new weapons to beat down the competition next year."

"It might be best we get in there and comfort the troops," my father suggested, his face debonair as he glanced at his GM.

The locker room was doleful. The press had been refused entry. The quiet of the space was eerie. Gus, our forty-year-old veteran, broke the silent gloom.

"That's it for me, boys. I'll be hanging up the cleats having never won the big one. But I want to say this was a hell of a ride. We all did our best and nobody will ever fault us for lack of heart. I'm proud to have been part of this group…every one of you should be too."

"Thanks, buddy," Flores yelled from his locker across the room. "What can you do? Saturdays are always the worst luck for me," he emphasized by slamming his fist into the door of his locker.

"It was my fault," Wilcox volunteered. "I was damned."

"That's bullshit, my friend," Carrillo challenged.

"No, you don't understand. I have to come clean. I have only one fear in life. Rodents give me the chills. You tell me why the damn thing was there, the only creature that could have rattled me—a bird could have crapped on my head and I wouldn't have flinched. It was

269

a rotten rodent curse, and I took all of you down with me," he lamented.

I listened to the players hashing over the series of events that led to losing the game. It was the same theme: one unexpected, unimaginable circumstance had the authority to change the currents of baseball history, and did it time and again. The only antidote known to the players that was considered to have a beast of a chance to tame the mercurial madness was ritual, some form of repeated supplication to the God of Mercy to spare them, if only momentarily from the ravaging waving wand of fortune.

Wilcox, the Holy Shit man of our team, the guy we plucked out of the hands of The Royals for pocket change, had a terrible fear of rodents. At just the instant he was to make the crucial catch, magic sent a menace rat to trip history onto its derriere. I thought if I were a businessman and wanted to make a bundle I'd get the recipe to Amos Hoskins' powder and brand it.

My father interrupted the sorrowful scene with a dose of reality.

"Can I have all of your attention, please? I want to share a story I'm not sure I've ever related, even to my son. I served in Viet Nam for two years. During my tour, I saved every dime I could and vowed that if I lived I'd use my stash to go into business for myself. When my service to my country ended, I came home and invested those dollars I had saved in a venture a friend was starting. He defrauded me out of every cent. Within a year, I was flat broke.

"Oh yes, I didn't give up. I had the brashness and poor judgment to go belly up two more times. On each of those occasions, I hurt so badly that I thought god was punishing me. I wanted to cry my way to Vegas. I probably would have, had I any money left to gamble. But in my heart I knew that wasn't the answer." He stopped to look around the room, making sure to make eye contact with everyone present. "Now I know there will be a lot of suffering during the off-season, and that's part of losing. I can't fix it for any of you."

Then he paused to look at Sky and me.

"Son, I think you figured out the lessons I meant for you to learn. You're not a baseball man but I'm proud of you as a man just the same. Sky, this is your baby. I'll leave it to you to run the team as you see fit. What you've done for this glorious sport is magnificent. Even my wife never squawks when I ask her to come to a game," he chuckled.

He waved to Sky to suggest it was her turn to address her crew. She jumped up on one of the benches so she could be seen clearly by the men.

"First of all, no weeping. We're set to make a big move next year." She took a piece of paper out of her pocket and read. "If The Blue Stripes finish the full season with a better win-loss record than The Rivals, they are entitled to any two players of their choosing from

271

The Rivals roster…this little note goes on to define the detail, fellows. What do you think about that? It's just the beginning of our ascent." She smiled proudly. "You guys did damn well."

"No, you did damn well," Rory, one of the few players remaining from our old club, countered her.

"Just did what any GM is paid to do, try to build a winner," Sky retorted.

"No, we're not idiots. We know we busted ourselves real hard but it was the music. We figured it out along the way," Rory laughed. "Still, it worked so what were we to do?"

"I'll just say this…and no more about music. We did our part and you did yours."

"We may have jumped ahead of ourselves," Rory continued, "but we assumed that at this moment we would be celebrating. So for the anticipated festivities we prepared a gift for all of you…boys, can we get into it?"

The room was still filled with doleful faces, hardly in the spirit to perform. But Rory stood his ground.

"Men, we owe it to them. We have lots of time to sulk later," he advised.

Gradually signs of affirmation were delivered through nods of heads and raised arms; the invitation seeming to lure them out of the funky state most wanted to hide in.

"This is for you Sky, Ben, Whit and Professor," Rory announced. "We call it, *The Finale*, but I'm thinking it's really better titled, *The Commencement*."

One of the members of the team started playing music. It was their composition and their lyrics; each had rehearsed their lines.

"We've put our hearts and pride into this year's wondrous ride, but no amount of drive would have been enough to get our team to thrive.

"Sure, we work 'til hustle tears us, far as our muscles dare us, but guts just ain't enough to get our team to flare up.

"We know we're critical and we did all of the things we ought, but hard work ain't enough, most times you need an extra pop.

"We work all year it's true but somewhere beyond our view the magic's got to brew or we'd be just as good as through.

"We've toiled, it's the truth, but ball teams are more than brutes. Without four jewels like you any team's as good as through.

"We've got our lucky trinkets, headless fish if you can think it, but all our little games don't quite explain why we ain't sinkin.'

"We're on the rise and what a high it's been the whole damn time to be a part of something perfectly in tune and rhyme.

"See, every player plays for just that special day but so much can block our way that half the time we simply pray.

"We work all year it's true, but somewhere beyond

our view the magic's got to brew or we'd be just as good as through."

Sky jumped in. It was as if she'd rehearsed her lines a hundred times but it was on the spot, spontaneous lyrics.

"We've paved a road to help this team to grow, we know it's true. Indeed, behind the magic brews...but you can do the same thing too. There's always something left, something sitting in the depths. We found our something new but you can do the same thing too."

She repeated the last line, *you can do the same thing too*, ten times. By the time she finished, the seven-word phrase was a chant, a sacred psalm.

*****

Almost two hours passed before we were notified that the stadium had emptied. We were all grateful when it was announced that there were no incidences of violence. The locker room gradually cleared out, the players, manager, coaches, batboys and other ancillary personnel having to face for themselves the sadness that could never be buried in a single pep talk.

My father left with Tollini, planning to go home and discuss their on-going business dealings. Sky, Whitman, Karlov and I were the only ones left. I couldn't help recounting as I glanced at my fellow actors staring in what I envisioned as a living play all the events that had occurred as a result of one act of deceit on the part of Thorne.

We had all changed. For the three males, we discovered the confidence to win in the game of romance. Whitman delighted in his harem of ravishing ladies, though over time he lost interest in playing the field and was cozying up to Kona on an exclusive basis. Karlov had transformed into a stud, at last living a dream-turned-dusty after years of dreary despair. Ben Wolf had found the lion's courage hiding in his meek heart and used it to woo the only girl he'd ever love; and he'd have grown into a man.

Sky too realized gains unanticipated. She had confronted demons of love-terror she'd rarely permitted herself to openly face, not to mention single-handedly transformed one of our country's greatest national treasures.

One afternoon shortly after the series ended, I was on my way to have lunch with my father, when one of his top executives, Harold Clancy, ran into me walking down the hall.

"Ben, you look great," he greeted me by wrapping his arms around me like I was a capo of a mafia crew.

He was a man I knew to be close to my father's age but neglect of his physique had puffed him out such that he reminded me of a lollipop, his upper body weighing heavily on his skinny long legs. There was no lack of strength in his hands, gripping my arms after the embrace.

"I remember you as a little boy standing next to dad. He's proud of you, Ben."

"He should be. I'm a chip off the old block," I responded.

"You could do worse, buddy boy. Few left in this world like Arnold Wolf." He stood for a moment in contemplation before continuing with a thought he was forming. "I think I'm the only one standing from the original group of executives. Your dad is famous for bringing in youth; the older he gets the younger he promotes."

"You're right," I responded. Clancy had made a point I'd never focused on consciously but should have recognized. "He's turned The Blue Stripes over to Sky and she's only a tad past twenty-one."

"He respects the drive, intellect and imagination— the willingness to risk—that young people bring to the table. Ben, he's made millionaires out of more people still not thirty than Microsoft has." He smiled kindly. "Look, I have to rush off but good to see you."

I smiled, watching as his stick legs hauled his heavy load of flesh down the hall.

As I thought about what Clancy had said, it made sense. Arnold Wolf wasn't only giving the next generation a chance, he was breathing new life into his own lungs through their presence—it was the perfect symbiosis, for my father a proven method for eternal youthfulness.

I proceeded toward my father's office. When I turned right in the hall, Sky was walking toward me. She breezed right past me without a word. I'd have thought she was peeved had she not left in her wake an indecipherable smile. That gesture nonplussed me just enough to order down my instinct to chase after her.

After lunch, I went back to our apartment and both Sky and Whitman were there.

"Ben, I'm leaving," Whitman informed me. "I'm moving in with Kona."

"I'm glad for you, Whit. I'm sure you've thought this through…I mean you are kind of young."

"Thanks, daddy, but I know love when I see it."

Sky was sitting on the sofa listening, still sporting the same inexplicable grin on her face I had seen earlier that day.

"Listen, I gotta run but I'll be back later." Whitman headed for the door but before exiting he called out to us. "I knew you two would grow old together."

Whitman left. It was Sky and I alone. It was silent for some time before I spoke.

"So, um, what do you want to do?"

"I want to have sex…then I want to get married."

"Didn't we already have sex?" I questioned curiously.

"Not the way I want to have sex. I want to get you in

shape, call it spring training; then we can settle down together."

"Sky…I mean I'm young?" I laughed.

"That's how I like my men."

"But what will happen when I get older?"

"I'll make believe."

"So…it's sex right now," I affirmed as I began unbuttoning my shirt.

"It's sex forever, Ben."

Sky was wearing a bathrobe, a fact I hadn't taken into account until that moment when she…

Folks, that about brings us to…

THE END

OTHER NOVELS COMPLETED AND UPCOMING BY

Dennis A Nehamen

Mistaken Enemy
Insatiable Hate
Mescalero Blood
Crushing Steel
Musicball
DOGMAi
The Making of A Madman
Juliette
The Greatest American Outlaw
Music and Murder
Crushing Dreams

ABOUT THE AUTHOR

Dennis A Nehamen, Ph.D. is a forensic and clinical psychologist who has authored novels, screenplays and musicals, including the award-winning musical *Wrapped*. He lives in Los Angeles with his wife and has two adult children.

www.ingramcontent.com/pod-product-compliance
Lightning Source LLC
Chambersburg PA
CBHW071247210626
46818CB00013B/219